Chocolate Ty
A NOVEL BY CHERYL SUTHERLAND

Chocolate Ty is a work of fiction. It is not intended to depict, portray or represent any particular real persons. All the characters, incidents, and dialogues are the products of the author's imagination and are not constructed as real. Any resemblance to actual events or persons living or dead is purely coincidental. This book is solely for entertainment purposes.

Copyright © 2006 by Platinum Peach Press, LLC. All rights reserved

No part of this book may be reproduced in any form or by any means including electronic, mechanical or photocopying or stored in a retrieval system without permission in writing from the publisher except by a reviewer who may quote a brief passage to be included in a review.

Photography Cover Graphic Design Artist:
D. Suave Productions 561.840.8098
Cover layout by: www.Mariondesigns.com
Interior Layout: www.rodhollimon.com
ISBN: 0-9776199-8-2

Published in the United States of America by
Platinum Peach Press, LLC

CHOCOLATE Ty

DEDICATION

This book is dedicated, first of all, to all the friends and family that we have lost over the years. We have lost more people due to senseless violence than any other majority race. It needs to STOP. We are killing mothers, daughters, sisters, aunts, fathers, sons, brothers, uncles and the list goes on. Try to promote non-violence; you will be the bigger person. To the people that we have lost please keep their memories alive and well. We miss you and love you.

To my friends and family working 9 to 5's or those who are in the federal correctional facilities, to those who aren't my friends or family, to those who ever had a dream or vision and to those who are on the grind who hustle from dawn to dusk...stay committed and focused.

JUST KEEPING IT REAL!

My Daily Prayer:

Cast your burdens upon the Lord,
and He shall sustain you:
He will never suffer the righteous to be moved.

Psalms 55:22

Acknowledgements

I would like to give an honor to my Heavenly Father for without him none of this would be possible. I would like to thank him for the blessings and talents that he bestowed upon me....

I would like to thank my mother, Irene, for the encouragement and help that she gave me when no one else would. I would like to thank my father, Lincoln, for keeping me in his thoughts and prayers. I would like to thank my sister, Sandra for letting me borrow some of your sanity when I lost all of mine.

To my girl Naimah, you don't know how much you helped me this year. I know that you have had your own trials and tribulations but you still made time for me. I love you for that, I respect you for that, and I thank GOD for you.

To my cousins Fay and Belinda I love y'all with all my heart and soul. Oh yeah and Fay thank you for busting out windows with me and Belinda being there for me when I needed the therapy.

To my Orange County Girls Chemeka B., Tomeika R. and Lekisha P. thank you for being my critics and "Big Sisters" when I needed you, except you Lekisha cause you don't really like me. (Smile).

To my little sister Erika thank you for being the surrogate mother to my daughter as well as being an awesome Godmother. I Love Ya!

To my P.I.H. (Partner In Hustling) Stephaney, Karja and the kids. I love y'all too. Thank you for believing in me.

To Keisha Dallas thank you for being my best friend even though we don't talk every day I still love you and I am going to marry your little brother, Kevin.

To Shavon holding it down in VA, thank you for believing in me when most people brushed me off for even having this dream.

To Jackie Williams, another VA affiliate, I know that you thought I wasn't going to be able to get you in but I did. I need some poetry girl. Help a sister out and stay a positive person and give my baby, Jasmine, all the kisses and hugs her auntie can't give right now. I love you.

To Miss Susie M. you know who you are and please stay that way.

To Oral thank you for being my friend first

and then a big brother and listening to me when others got tired.

To LL it was nice meeting you and I appreciate the opportunity to get to know you and your insights and thoughts about life. It will help me with the next novel.

To Jarrod, Dread, Shawn and Big Head Mike (MJ) thank you for the inspiration, tough love and some of the advice and criticism that you gave me. It really helped.

To my "Big Brothers" at Big Scale Entertainment keep doing what y'all do because IT IS working!!!

To **Platinum Peach Press**, thank you for this opportunity to be a part of your movement.

Last but definitely not the least D. Suave thanks for designing my book cover.

To all the HATERS I would like to thank you for being haters and making me strive even more to be successful and accomplishing my goals in life.

Now, to my beloved ANGEL Kamilyn, I would like to thank you the most. You gave me strength when I didn't have any left. Just a look into your eyes gave me the passion to complete many tasks. I truly and deeply love you with all my heart. Thank You.

To everyone else that I forgot to name, I'm sorry, but you know who you are and you are near and dear to my heart.

    Keep ya' head up, we on the map.

My Stranger

If you touch me there I shiver
If you kiss me there I quiver
Imagine if we were in love
Such a beautiful thing
To smile everyday and make our hearts sing
It's like the sunshine after the storm
It could be 20 degrees outside and I'll still be warm
Happiness is the main reason why I want to live
We're mad when we fight but happy when we forgive
Call me sometime, maybe we can talk
Or even stop by maybe we can go for a walk
Hold my hand, tell me what you feel
Is this how it is? Does this feel real?
Is that a smile I see? I told you it feels good
You fronted on my abilities when you knew I could
I want to get to know you better
Is that okay with you?
I want to get to love you more
And hope you love me too
So what's the deal with you
Let me know something, honey
I'm feeling you real hard but you actin' kind of funny
So get yourself together and when you do get it right
Take the time to think about me and holla back
tonight. ~

The thoughts of Jackie Williams

PRELUDE

It was another hot, sunny afternoon in West Palm Beach, Florida. Sweat was drizzling down the middle of my breasts as the palm trees whistled in the breeze like a perfectly harmonized orchestra. I waited outside of Palm Beach Gardens High School for my ride to come pick me up from school. I noticed a handsome guy on the other side of the breezeway. He was about six-feet tall with a muscular build and dreads, I couldn't really see his face but by his silhouette alone he had my attention.

I observed his surroundings and noticed a car in which I stared at because it was one that I have seen many times before parked at this establishment but never distinguished who owned the vehicle. It was a luxury car with very dark tints and shiny rims. I caught myself staring at him and quickly turned my head as he detected me watching him. I kept my head straight forward as I observed him through my peripheral vision. He was amazing in my eyes; I felt such an attraction towards him as if it was love at first sight. But all my thoughts were distorted when I saw a stocky butch-like woman walking in my direction, so I took my focus off of him and looked at my watch to see what time it was.

The woman came closer and I began to feel nauseous for some reason. She came and stood right next to me.

"Excuse me do you have the time?"

"Yes. It's 2:40." I answered nervously.

"My brother wants to know if you have a ride or would you like him to take you home, since you're staring so hard?"

"Excuse me? Who is your brother?"

"The one you been over here sweating and acting like you don't want to come over there and converse with."

She pulled my card. I really wanted to go but I don't ride with strangers. At that point I saw my friend Cheryl walking in the direction of the entourage. Cheryl stood about five-feet even, she had about a 32B breast size, greenish brown eyes, and a very nice behind. Hell, her shape was phenomenal something that most of the Jamaican girls had in common. She had all the females hating because she was a track star at our school and never dated any of the jitterbugs that attended Palm Beach

Cheryl Sutherland

Gardens High. Some people called her stuck up but I called her my friend, and I could not believe that she knew this fine ass stranger and never said anything to me. I felt betrayed over this stranger. I didn't know him from Adam and here I am getting upset. I watched as she gave the tall statuesque stranger a hug.

My blood started to boil as if this guy and I were together for years. He leaned over and tapped the side of the car as another guy opened the door from the inside. It was Cheryl's boyfriend Terrance, he stepped out surrounded by a cloud of smoke. His eyes were red and low which were halfway covered by his reddish-brown dreads. He was a shorty in my book with a height of 5'5" and he weighed about 200 even, I think he used to play football for one of our rival schools. All the colleges wanted him and so did the girls. He was a hot commodity within the teenage genre but Cheryl was his #1 draft pick.

Cheryl ran and gave him a kiss.

"Are you coming or are you going to be a spectator?" the stranger asked me.

"Um, let me find out about this with my homegirl."

"Who are you talking about? Cheryl? She's cool. Girl come on, you a trip. What you scared? We ain't gonna bite." She giggled.

We walked over to the car and Cheryl walked towards me. I didn't know what she was going to say but I bet it had to do with my secret crush. She wrapped one arm around my neck and began to whisper in my ear. She told me his name was the infamous Tilak Masters, a nigga that you always hear about but never see.

Cheryl claimed that he got so much money and that he wasn't stingy. She gave me a quick synopsis on him that managed to keep me interested. She explained about the "business" that he was in and that it was very profitable. Now Cheryl was in high school along with me but knew everything going on outside of school.

She told me how he owned an automobile transporting business that he and his father created, she told me that he never was caught with a girl on his arm because he was just too fine to have any old girl by his side; she told me how he needed a *ride-or-die* chick or someone very similar.

At that moment I knew that was not me, but maybe I can learn a thing or two from just being around him. Cheryl then interrupted my thought by concluding her synopsis of Tilak by saying:

"Girl you might as well get in and learn the game a little bit, shit you might as well let him mold

Cheryl Sutherland

you into his likeness. In other words *GET PAID!*"

Everything sounded good but was I ready for an older guy, one that is so established, fine and eloquent. I was nervous as hell and Cheryl wasn't making it any better. I stopped in my tracks and told Cheryl that I couldn't talk to him. She saw the embarrassment and nervousness in my face and she encouraged me to do it because he was a hot catch and all the girls in school would be envious of me. So I sucked up all my meekness and shyness and let the words "GET PAID" echo in my head over and over again.

Walking closer to him I critiqued myself, analyzing my best qualities and eliminating from my mind the flaws that I have and replaced them with more pleasant thoughts. Hell, I was cute, petite and single, what more could I want out of my premature life than a fine man with his own whip and loot. So I got up the nerve and approached him. I tucked my hair behind my right ear and I stuck out my left hand and introduced myself.

He grabbed my hand and pulled me closer to him, he embraced me as if he didn't want to let me go. He planted a kiss on my forehead, my body started to form goose bumps all over and my private part started to tingle. I knew that this was it. I felt it in my heart.

―――――――――― Chocolate Ty ――――――――――

He asked me if I was ready to go and I nodded my head in agreement.

He walked me over to my door and opened it for me, as I sat on the passenger side of his car he whispered in my ear, "You're gonna love me."

I couldn't help but smile.

That day we rode and listened to music in his 1997 Mercedes Benz S500. The car's system was banging, and all of our backs were vibrating. I couldn't imagine myself doing this all the time it just wasn't me.

That's when I was introduced to the soon-to-be love of my life…weed. Cheryl and Terrance was rolling and the blunts were being passed in rotation. I passed on the first couple of offers but after I caught a contact it was all over. Tilak was warning me that when most people smoke for the first time they are paranoid and confused, so if I start to get dizzy or got a cotton mouth that I should stop until I come down off my high for a little bit. But I smoked all of them under the table and after that day they made fun of me, calling me lil' Hoover.

As the days went by Tilak and I became really close really quick. I was scared a little bit because this was my first time ever getting into a relationship this serious and exciting. Hell, this was my first relationship period. I mean I wasn't a virgin but I was never committed to anyone either.

He really had me thrown (confused) because I was living with Tilak by the first month of us being together and from my recollection he didn't want to be seen in public with a chick let alone have them living with him.

I did not complain.

He would come home sometimes 2 or 3 o'clock in the morning and wake me up out of my sleep to count garbage bags full of money.

I did not complain.

While he rested I would count thousands of dollars, sometimes I wouldn't finish until it was time for me to go to school. He would be sleeping and I would be counting.

Still I did not complain.

The urge to steal from him crossed my mind plenty of times but I knew that it wasn't worth it. I would ask him, "why don't you just buy a money counting machine?" But he would just give me a look like I was crazy and answer me, "You are my money counting machine," and give me a kiss on the forehead.

All the things that I was doing for him weren't reciprocated. I thought that he wasn't taking care of me like I thought he should have but what could I say, I wasn't out there getting money like he was, it was his dough and if I wanted my own I would have to work for it just like he did. Matter of fact it was exciting counting all that dough because more likely than not I wouldn't see that much money at one time if I was single so I did my job, a job that he trusted me with.

By the third month he had me going to school at home and had me working for him by the time I got my diploma. Me working for him didn't last long at all. He always used to think that every man wanted me, which seemed kind of weird because EVERYONE knew that we were together. He made me stop working there anyways.

He hired this chick named Lisa, who was a very jealous person, to be his receptionist. I only saw her once, but spoke with her on many occasions when I called the office. She always had a little hostility in her voice when it came to me. She would lie and say that Tilak wasn't there but when I called his cell phone he would say that he was at the office, so I don't know what stunt she was trying to pull but it wasn't cool. I erased her out of my mind to the point that if she was standing next to me I would not have known who she was.

A year later Tilak set me up in my own apartment saying that he needed a little space. That was cool, the same thoughts were in my head but I didn't dare to bring them to my lips. Tilak had me in a nice ass apartment on Village Boulevard...miles away from the bullet- ridden streets and hourly sounds of the police sirens of Blue Heron Boulevard. He set me up in a gated community off of Brandywine Road, it was a one bedroom and one bathroom apartment, which we both decorated because he has very good taste. Tilak had my place laid out with very nice things but it didn't compare to his house that he occupied or the plans of the other house that he was going to have built from the ground up. My thoughts were that we will be living together again after that house is built but I will take advantage of what I have now while I have it.

I quickly gained a lot of attention from being Tilak's girl. He and I started to show our faces in public together. Any and every main function that happened we were there, looking like a perfectly matched pair. I guess the months of not complaining finally paid off. He had me spoiled and everyone knew it. We were hood rich, ghetto celebrities. We couldn't take two steps without having to shake hands with somebody or giving hugs, daps or high five's.

I would get stares from chicks who wanted to be in my shoes or who had secretly been in my shoes. I would get stares from niggas trying to plot on how to get a chick like me on their team if not me. I was always fly, two steps ahead of the game. Things that I wore girls would always ask, "Oh, where did you get that from? Or Damn girl you rocking that Chanel," or whatever designer brand I had on that day. That made me feel like I was above everybody in Riviera. I know that there was hate in the air but nobody would step to the plate.

When it came to dudes, I mean I had other guys no doubt, but living alone had made me mature very quickly, knowing what it takes to maintain "on my own". I knew that other guys would come in handy…you know just in case purposes. But having Tilak as a boyfriend helped out a lot, my guy friends always looked out, or thought that they were helping but Tilak kept me on an allowance of $1500.00 a week, faithfully, which worked for me.

I had a 1998 Mercedes Benz that was paid for, thanks to Tilak and his cousin. He wanted everyone to know that my car was mine and I was his, so he made our cars customized to look alike. Tilak had my car painted black with dark tints, he put 20' inch rims on it, something that was very rare for a chick to have back then, he had ABC Customs re-do the interior with a custom made grey and black leather Gucci material, and all Pioneer sound system.

I even had customized plates that read MSTRS which stood for his last name. Tilak paid my $800 a month rent for my apartment and he was paying my bills. Those other dudes couldn't manage all that, that's why I gave them nothing but conversation and kept everything for my man. Maintaining my living quarters and keeping my man happy was the only thing that I was actually obligated to do by Tilak and that's what I did.

I was so caught up in this life of paradise that I hadn't been focusing on me and what I mean by that is my future. I called Cheryl to get a little advice and she advised me that I needed to start saving my money so that if anything goes wrong between Tilak and myself that I would be able to live off of the money that I had saved, which made sense to me so I started to do so.

I opened a bank account that Tilak knew nothing about and started putting a thousand dollars in it every week. I had money stashed everywhere. At the house, in the bank, in my jeans pockets, under the mattress, in safes and in cookie jars. I felt as if I was a part of the "Beverly Hillbillies" like I had struck oil and didn't know how to act. I couldn't even say that I was still the same Tyrena. I never knew life could be so sweet and simple until things got complicated...

CHAPTER 1

"What do you mean you gotta go! That's all I've been getting from you Tilak! I only see your back now! All you do is go, go, go. Shit, I have half the mind to...hello? HELLO! I know this mutha-fucker did not hang up on me again! Fuck this!" I said as I got my keys to go jump in my brand new Lexus truck.

I had to calm down because I was very accident prone if I drove when I was mad. That's how I wrecked both of my Benz's so I prayed and got focused before I got on the road. Still the thoughts were in my head and nothing but words played in my mind. Thoughts, situations and instances were all that occupied my brain.

"All my years on this blessed earth and I can't begin to fathom what I've done wrong to deserve this. From my point of view, this relationship has been totally one sided for the past year and now, out of all things, I'm about to be a mother. I can't believe this shit. This definitely can't be happening to me.

My mother told me to be a lady about the situations I encounter in life but right now this nigga just persists on trying me. I mean he treats me alright and all but he still has other women out there. I'm no dummy. A man as fine as Tilak…humph, he got to have other hos. But I'm his main girl. See here I go again rambling on to myself. Since I've been with Tilak a lot has changed. I mean I've changed, I've became a woman. I've done a lot of growing up and now is the time to present this to him." I said gathering my thoughts.

I was the type of person that always overanalyzed circumstances. I would think things through as long as I wasn't upset. If I got upset then all that logic went out the window.

"You know what, fuck it!" I interjected; "I'm young, intelligent and beautiful. That's something the rest of his bitches will never have over me. I don't have to take nothing this nigga dishes out. He knows that now I'm only with him for his money" I joked. I looked around to see if anyone saw me talking to myself out loud.

"It's bad because I lost respect for him a long time ago but my mind is still fucked up about him.

Chocolate Ty

I don't know what I'm gonna do about this seed growing in my womb. What am I gonna do? I guess when I swing by his house we can discuss the whole situation. We can weigh our options and come to some sort of resolution. I just hope things don't get blown out of proportion... Literally!"

I sat at the stop sign and tapped my fingers on the steering wheel until I convinced myself that this was something that had to be dealt with today.

"I guess I'll spend a couple of hours with the love of my life Mr. Tilak. I hope he takes this as good news. I mean I know that I'm not ready for a shorty but we gotta do what we gotta do. If he feels that he's not ready it will make everything a whole lot easier."

I convinced myself.

CHAPTER 2

When I pulled into the driveway I just had to smile. I looked at his house as an accomplishment. He's the only nigga I ever fucked with that owned his home. I knew that I was doing big things when I started messing with this cat, I assured myself. I continued boasting while parking the truck.

"I got a man with a two story house, with the foliage trimmed perfectly to accent the beige exterior of the home. His house over looks the ocean that always seems so peaceful and serene. And across the bluish green water is a city that I don't even know the name of."

I walked to the house reminiscing on the love we made while on the terrace. I was deep in thought, prancing towards the garage entry. It was as if I was dancing on cloud nine. He's the only one who could do this to me. Undeniably, Tilak was my everything no matter how I tried to slice it and I loved that...I loved him.

―――――――――――― Cheryl Sutherland ――――――――――――

Deep in the back of my mind I knew that he wasn't faithful but I had no evidence of unfaithfulness. He kept his pimpin' on lock, he was never caught slipping. I smiled to myself as I thought back on how the inside of Tilak's domain remained. I reminisced on how the Italian furniture nestled us as we watched movies and the white mink rugs that we used to have sex on always were a comfort to me. I loved the mink rugs because it never gave me rug burns and I liked to wiggle my cute, neat manicured toes in it. The mink rugs covered the marble floors; the marble floors matched the marble embedded dining room table and countertops.

Tilak made sure that he had the best of the best. He had china and crystal. He had silverware that was actually made out of silver, cloths and throws from Egypt, decorative paintings and those exotic ostrich eggs that cost mad money. Of course last but not least he had a 62 inch plasma television with a Bose surround sound. It always felt as if we were in the theatres.

I walked into the garage and admired Tilak's 2003 gold Jaguar on 22 inch rims, that was his birthday present to himself, he was proud of his upgrade from a Benz to Jaguar and next is a Porsche. But for now his Jaguar was the ride of all rides down in Palm Beach. It has custom Alligator skin interior that he had dyed to match the color of his car, TV's all in the headrests, doors and in the floors of the car and don't forget a matching Alligator convertible top. His customized Florida tag read Tilak.

The thoughts of his car started to make me wet, I always imagined riding up the coast naked with the top down and wheels spinning. I just wanted to take my clothes off and run in his house and surprise him, but with my luck all his homeboys would be in there. That's why I'm in the predicament I'm in now…PREGNANT.

"I think I'll give him a lil' sump tin' before I break the news to him about his shorty. I know that I'm gonna want an abortion and I know that he may trip but what can I say, I'm only 20 and I know that I'm not ready for a baby. Shit, I'm too stuck on me having the best for me rather than sharing my money and time on another human being."

I walked up to the garage.

"What's the code for this stupid garage?" I typed in the numbers 8-7-1-9-8-0…beep, beep, beep sounded the garage alarm as it opened its doors.

As soon as the door opened I saw a car that I didn't recognize, an Oldsmobile Aurora. I ran through all of his friends and their whips in my head and couldn't connect any of his friends with this particular car.

"Who the fuck car is this?" I thought to myself, "I really hope its one of his homies 'cause I'm not even with this today."

I proceeded to the door that's always unlocked and what do you know, today of all days the door is locked. I heard the thumping of bass and gave myself a crazy look.

"Why is he playing his music so loud? He must be in there with his homeboys trying to show out. I bet this mother fucker don't even know that I have the keys to his shit. I got keys to his cars, house, apartments, front doors, back doors, boats, safes and locks, I mean everything."

I ran the thought through my mind.

I stopped in my tracks trying to reassure myself that he was not in there with the bullshit. The thought of him being in there with another girl briefly ran across my mind. I shook it off because I knew that his game is tighter than that. Plus I knew that going to jail today was not on my agenda. I started talking to myself trying to calm myself down.

"Alright girl, Tilak does think that you are a LADY so try to behave like one. Try not to act ignorant but be firm, be assertive so he knows that you're not playing. Okay her we go." After the pep

Chocolate Ty

talk I tip-toed back to my candy blue 2002 Lexus RX 300 on 24' rims.

I reached down into the compartment under the passenger seat and removed the correct color coded key. My palms were sweating and there were butterflies in my stomach as well as a lump in my throat. I quickly grabbed the key and power walked back to the garage door. I stuck the key in the lock and slowly unlocked the door. I heard him talking and laughing, just having a good old time. I really couldn't hear anyone responding so I knew at that point and time that he wasn't chillin' with his loud and boisterous homeboys. The anger grew inside of me like a wildfire. All I could think about was leaving and going straight to Presidential Woman's Clinic to abort his child.

I crept in making sure that Tilak wouldn't see me. I paused as he carried his guest upstairs. I followed him as soon as he bent the corner to go to his master bedroom. I started to prowl behind them; the way I moved up the stairs was cat-like, very quiet and very subtle. I paused when I reached the top of the staircase. I looked at him and his company through the mirrored walls in the hallway.

I watched as the chick put on some sort of strip show for him. The chick was at least 6 foot 2 and she had long black weave that reached the middle of her back. She had tattoos galore. Her body was okay but I had her beat. She looked ridiculous trying to be seductive and sexy and she's built like a dude. I thought of that as being in the *"on-the-down-low"* category but never minded it. I watched as each article of clothing fell to the floor.

I sat back as the sharp pains in my stomach made me fold over. I felt a little nausea being bestowed upon me by the actions that were being performed by this girl. I got on my knees and watched the rest of the show. I watched as the Amazon chick walked over to Tilak in some banging ass stilettos and grinds her naked body against him.

She began to kiss him...in his mouth...and he let her. She kissed his neck and took his shirt off. She began to kiss his chest, taking time with each nipple flicking her tongue over each areola making sure that they were standing erect before she moved over to the other.

She slid her tongue down his six-pack and began to kiss his navel and un-button his pants at the same time. I felt the tears swell up in my eyes as I turned away in disbelief. I now knew what type of person Tilak really was. A hundred thoughts were going through my mind. I turned back and looked as I saw my man standing there naked.

I couldn't believe my eyes when this ho went

down on my man.

This girl has a deep throat, Tilak is a Mandingo, and he hangs nine-inches when he's not even aroused and at least 12-inches when he is. This ho was taking his whole cock in her mouth, at attention, with room to spear. Hell, I couldn't even get mad 'cause I would gag just trying to get it in just past the head. The stranger looked Tilak dead in the eyes as she got off on his penis. Tilak eyes left hers and rolled into the back of his head.

That meant that he was enjoying every minute of it. Streams of tears started to roll down my face. I wondered if the thought of me even ran through his mind while he was getting major head from this broad. I could tell that it was getting good to him because he grabbed her hair and helped her bring him to that spot he likes to reach.

Tilak stopped her and told her to get up off her knees and walk to the chair. He took his "chick of the day" and carried her to the chaise lounge chair that he had in his room. He instructed her to bend over and placed his unprotected penis into her vagina from behind.

He started off slow making sure that she can take it. As soon as he saw that it was all good he started to pick up the pace.

By this time I was mentally insane. The

psychotic part of my brain was telling me to bust up in the motherfucker but the sane part wanted him to get his rocks off first.

"Auugghhnn, damn this pussy so good baby," Tilak was yelling, "ummph I love you girl. This my pussy ain't it. Throw that pussy back at me."

She was saying back to him, "Take this pussy, it's yours. Beat it up, baby...ooohh shit I'm bout to cum. Smack my ass, Tilak. Grab it, augghhnn!" she moaned.

The disturbing and menacing plots that I was concocting had ceased by the voices of my man and another woman engaging in intercourse. I was literally sitting on my hands to keep myself from jumping up and beating his ass. Hell, by the time I finished my thoughts it was over. He came all over her; his sperm was on her back and ass.

The baby that was growing in me had his future brothers and sisters all on her. I shook my head and tried to get it together because it was going down.

He sat down and grabbed a towel off the back of the chair. The girl looked at him and asked him if he wanted to go at it again. He denied her request and told her to get up and start the shower. He wiped his dick off and jumped up to go into the master bathroom. This was the perfect opportunity for me to get messy.

I walked into the bedroom and sat on the bed. I looked around the room and saw all the scattered clothing randomly placed on the floor. The tears were coming in abundance. I wanted to fucking kill him.

All I wanted to do was tell him that he had a baby on the way and this is what I get? I thought to myself, *I don't even know what to do.*

I tried to gain my composure as I heard the shower turn off. I kept standing and sitting not being sure of which one to do. Tilak walked in first as we locked eyes. A stunned look came over his face, he was speechless. I stood up and did all the communicating for him. All I had to do was say four words that made him know that I wasn't playing. I slowly walked up to him with my hands behind my back and eyed the girl from over his shoulder. I got right in his face and said, "She needs to leave" and tried to walk off. Tilak grabbed my arm and asked me where I was going. I looked at my arm where his hand lay and gave him a look that can kill.

"What? You expect me to sit here and wait for your ugly, big ass, no titties having, zebra print thighs, big-eyed bitch to get dressed after she just got finished sucking my man up. Well I'm not going to do it! You need to get rid of her and I will be in my room, thinking of what to do about this."

"Baby it's not what you think." Tilak said.

"I know it's not what I think because it's what I saw. What the hell is this Tilak? I know that you know that I'm better than this. I am your woman and you can turn around and do me like this? Tilak GET RID OF HER!!!" I yelled with all the strength I had inside.

I turned and gave one last glance to both of them. I wanted to fucking kill them. I mean I wanted to load a gun and shoot them between the eyes. I could feel my hazel eyes glowing from the anger that had built up inside me. I opened my soft thin lips to utter the words that I anticipated will linger in his head for the rest of the day.

"I hope that you're happy with her 'cause I don't even want to fuck around with you like that, you bastard!" I walked away and a tear ran down my milk chocolate toned face.

I went into my quite room in the house. I lay on the bed as tears poured out of the corners of my eyes, wetting my silky black hair and the suede comforter. I started to countdown backwards from ten because I knew that Tilak will be there in a little bit.

A few seconds later there was a knock on the solid oak door. He cracked the door open and peeped in. "Bay, can I talk to you for a minute?" He asked.

"It's your house, Tilak," I replied nonchalantly.

He walked in with just a polo towel wrapped around him. He was still a little damp from the shower. His body was perfectly sculpted and his skin was just as black as it wanna be. You know the smooth, sexy, scrumptious, Morris Chestnut black. I couldn't believe it but my pussy was wet. This nigga was so fine I wanted to fuck the shit out of him right then and there, but I knew better even though I didn't want to.

"Bay, I know how much you care for me and all but I don't know if I'm ready to settle down to just one female. You gotta feel where I'm comin' from, boo." He said reluctantly since he knew that I was 'bout to flip the script in 3.2 seconds.

I sat up in the bed to make sure that I could amplify my voice.

"Is the bitch still in the house?"

"No", he responded with his head hung down, as I continued.

"Why would you do me like this? We've been together since I was 16 and that was 4 years ago. You know me and you know what I would do for you and to you. I'm not one of those hood rat bitches who shake they ass in the club every night that the clubs are open. Tilak I've been good to you. I've never cheated or disrespected you." I perjured. "I don't fuck with your homies and I make sure your punk ass is taken care of. All I get in return is you getting caught up with a long lipped, no shape having bitch and you're trying to tell me that it's not what it looks like as if I'm blind as hell. Nigga my vision 20/20. Oh yeah to add insult to injury you gonna tell me that you don't think that you ready to settle down with me?"

I stood up and walked around in a circle and mumbling to myself. "This nigga got to think that I'm a dummy, he just got to think that I'm stupid."

I guess I was making him nervous because the next thing I heard was him telling me to have a seat.

"Man sit down! Don't nobody think of you in that way. Don't nobody think you're stupid." I just giggled to myself because I knew that he was full of shit. I looked Tilak in the eyes and said the words that would cut deep into his soul.

"That's right I'm not stupid, you are, for trying me like this. You don't know shit about that girl yet you round here raw dogging her. That ho could be dying from HIV or AIDS, she could have a million kids and trying to set you up to be her next baby daddy, you fucking dummy. For all I know she could be a fucking psycho."

Chocolate Ty

    I kept in mind from the past, when he got caught up in petty lies, on how his eyes and body language would tell his true story. I could tell that he already knew this girl. So I walked up to him and looked at him as if he was a total stranger.

    "You already knew this broad huh? You been fucking this bitch haven't you? Answer me Tilak. You fucking her telling her how good her pussy is and that you love her. Do you love her Tilak, do you?" Tilak stood up and looked me in the eyes, he rubbed my shoulders and whispered…

    "Ty, I love you. I hope you understand that. I really don't see me going a day without you in my life. Hell, I know that I can't go a day without you in my life. A day without that smile that's so perfect and innocent. I love seeing that everyday." Tilak said with his hand on my chin gently rubbing my face hoping that it will calm me down a little bit since I loved hearing about my porcelain white teeth.

    "Don't try that shit with me!" I said snatching his hand away from my face "You fucked up, point blank, and you fucked her without a condom. Oh you definitely fucked up. I wonder what would've happened if I didn't catch you today. We probably would've fucked here tonight and kept it moving huh? I'm right aren't I?" Tilak just gazed up at the ceiling as if he was anticipating on me shutting my mouth.

I walked back around the bed to be opposite of him and read him like a book.

"I wish I never met your black ass in the first place. You ain't shit but another notch under my belt. I can do better than you. You ain't nothing but a paymaster to me. I hate you." I was steady going off on Tilak. I was so wrapped up in hurting him the way that he had hurt me that I didn't become aware of him creeping up on me.

Tilak never saw Tyrena in this way before but he's never been caught cheating before either. All he could think about is the way he used to keep her so near and dear to his heart. He was willing to die for her and she turns around and talks to him like he was a fucking stranger in the streets. He felt his blood boiling, his breath was falling short, and he couldn't even hear what she was saying anymore. It was as if his head had begun to submerge under water. Ty was steady going off on him. Talking bout how she can find a better nigga than him. She was snapping her fingers and rolling her neck. She boasted on how anyone would be willing to take care of her with no problems. She started crying because she knew she was telling the truth and he knew it too but he knew that she didn't want to leave him. The relationship was already established and she could get anything she wanted from him just by asking. He knew that she really didn't want to start over again.

In all honesty I really didn't want to leave, but I had to let him know that he hurt me and how much, I started to get hysterical. I turned and looked at him and uttered, "Who the fuck are you looking at, you clocking me as if I did something wrong, you punk ass nigga!"

All Tilak could do is hold his breath. She was getting the best of him and he was about to break. She pushed his buttons and knew it. The harder he tried to fight it the more his anger built. In a split second he pushed her so hard that she lost her balance and before she could regain it she caught a right hook in her mouth that sent her flying in the air and falling to the floor. Tilak pounced on top of her and was preaching to her while rearranging her face, telling her how much he loves her and how no other female was gonna take her place as well as no other nigga taking his. He stood up and started kicking her in the chest and stomach. He started stomping her legs and kept kicking her. Ty was in total shock, she couldn't believe that this nigga was unmercifully beating her. She then started to think about the life of her child, and tried to gain the strength to get up. Tilak grabbed her from off the floor by her hair. He then gripped around her arms tightly and began to shake her so violently that she thought her neck was about to snap.

I thought to myself, this nigga is beating the shit out of me, now I definitely know that I wasn't about to have his baby if I couldn't put an end to this violence. My only option was to let him know about the pregnancy so I yelled out to Tilak, "Stop, please stop shaking me. Tilak I'm pregnant. Let me go. Let me go!" I sobbed.

In all the rage it didn't register to Tilak what Tyrena had said. He continued to slap Ty in her face until she pulled away from his one handed grip. She ran towards the stairs and he was right behind her. Ty could hardly catch her breath. She saw blood on her clothes and stepped it up a notch. She tripped and fell down the last 4 steps slamming her body onto the floor face first. She balled herself into a fetal position as Tilak came running down after her. He picked her up by her forearms like a 30lb child. At that moment Ty had to do something to get out of his grips. She leaned her head back and head butted him with all her might. He let her go as she snatched *the towel from around him and ran out the kitchen door and outside into the garage. She fumbled to get in to the truck. She looked back at the garage and saw him standing there naked. Ty was glad that she left her keys in the truck. She threw the truck into reverse and peeled out.*

I could barely see where I was going with the combination of blood and tears in my eyes. Then my cell phone started to ring. It was him. As badly as I wanted to answer the phone I didn't. I flew through a stop sign almost hitting some kids that were playing in the street. I heard some sirens go off behind me but couldn't come to my senses quick enough to pull over. I was shook but slowly calmed down after the voice of the police officer rang out through the intercom.

I slowed the truck down and pulled over to the side of the road. I put the car in park and just cried and cried as the officer approached my truck. The police officer came towards the SUV and tapped on the window. I slowly raised my head to face the officer not even knowing what I looked like. The officer frowned in disgust and asked me what happened. I rolled the window down and came up with the quickest story that I could. I looked towards the officer and told him everything that happened but instead of Tilak being the culprit I blamed it on the chick that was at his house.

The officer shook his head in disbelief as he asked me if I wanted him to call an ambulance. I definitely agreed to that.

As we sat there and waited Officer Bullard began to make friendly conversation with me, telling me how beautiful I am and that I should never let any man get me into a situation like that. He brushed my hair with his fingers out of my face and preached about life I quickly thought about what life would be like if I was to get with a man like him, a man on the straight and narrow. I snapped back into reality to hear him say.

"Life is too short, you should live it to the fullest and be thankful for It." he added. I just agreed by nodding my head because I didn't want to hear that shit right now.

After I heard the sirens for the ambulance I looked up and saw Tilak drive by in his Jaguar with the look of Satan in his eyes. At that point I knew it wasn't over. I knew there was more to come. It was going to be the war between lovers and I damn sure was determined to win this battle.

CHAPTER 3

"Three months have gone by and no abortion was needed since Tilak beat his child out of me" I thought to myself. "All I have is an emptiness inside, where my child should've been growing. I haven't been able to look at another man. Tilak got me messed up in the head. I've been by myself ever since. I can't trust no nigga. I had to change my apartment buildings and downgrade to this shit hole. I had to change my cell and house number. Hell I've been imprisoned in my own shit because of this fool, but today I am going to release myself" I said looking outside my apartment window.

I stared at the corner store across the street as I saw someone to my liking. A young black man walked into the store. I hopped up and threw on a sweat suit and some AF1's and hauled ass to the store to catch up with this stranger.

"I'm cute again, I know I can pull him I mean I don't need him but I'm so lonely and I need some sort of "company" even if it lasts for only a month or two." I said to prep myself up.

The stranger was walking out the store by time I got there. I made him bump into me as I looked at him and excused myself while I twisted my way past him. Of course he turned around to see what I was working with. He licked his lips and rubbed his hands together as he followed me to the refrigerator that held the Capri- suns. I grabbed a Pacific Cooler and ran into him again.

"Damn I'm gonna have to get insurance if we keep running into each other like this." I giggled.

"What's yo' name lil' momma." the stranger asked.

"Ty, what's yours?" I said.

"Yeah, my name Vint. You from round here?" he asked with his gold teeth shining. He has the cutest smile I have ever seen I thought to myself. He's so fine with his low haircut; his edge is sharp as hell. He a lil' fat but I definitely can work with that. Shit his Nike's even clean. Girbuad from head-to-toe, damn what's a girl to do?

"Uh, yeah, I stay right there in those apartments." I pointed towards the wall that separated my apartments from the convenient store. "Why, where you from?" I asked inquisitively.

"I'm from Georgia, but I stay down off 2nd

street for now." he said with a smirk on his face.

"Oh, off of Old Dixie." I said in a know-it-all tone of voice.

"Yep," Vint said as he paid for my Capri- sun

"So can I come check you or do you have an old man" Vint said looking down my sweat suit jacket.

"If I did have a man he wouldn't be down my jacket in between my right and left breast." I said with a smile, "But no, me and my ex, his name Tilak, we broke up three months ago." Vint looked at me kind of strange, I guess he heard that name before. Vint asked me for my number and I gave it to him. As I walked away he told me he would call me. I bet it up.

Vint jumped into his ride as he thought about how good she could be in bed. The thought of him being inside of her just boggled his mind, he wanted to make it a reality. He broke out of his fantasy as his cell phone rang, it was his homeboy Flick.

"What up nigga." Vint expressed.
"Shit dog, wassup wit you?" Flick responded.
"Man I just met this fine ass female by the name of Ty. Man she flyer than a motherfucker but she used to fuck with Tilak though. I know I ain't

supposed to but, she's mine." Vint said.

"Dog, you know you playing with fire. All the hos Tilak fucked with are some conceited ass bitches. He give them the world and that's all they gonna expect from here on out. Don't do it. I'm telling you don't do it."

"I hear ya though. I'm a holla back at you in a few."

"Yeah, hurry up I got that work nigga." *Vint hung up the phone and gave Ty a call.*

I got the call soon after I left the store. It was my new found friend checking to see if that was the right number that I given him. I laughed to myself as I thought, "Damn niggas still do shit like that. Hell if I didn't want to give him the right number I wouldn't have gave him one at all." I answered the phone and confirmed a date for that night at 9 p.m.

I walked back to my apartment to grab some snacks from on top of the refrigerator so I could go downstairs to my "homegirl" Pat's apartment to tell her about my new found friend. I got all the way to Pat's door and forgot the hot sausages that Pat love to smack on. I turned and made my way back up the stairs. When I got to the 3rd floor I saw him standing right in front of my door. I nearly peed on myself as Tilak turned towards my direction not even noticing me. I slowly walked back down the stairs to my girlfriends' apartment on the second floor. I lightly tapped on the door with my keys and Pat hurried to the door because she knew what time it was.

Now Pat was a very unique individual, her real name was Patrick, you know a woman trapped in a man's body, but she can play it off real well, especially since she was on hormone therapy. She didn't look like a guy at all. She had nice legs, a feminine voice, a small Adams apple, nice breasts, a flat stomach, and a round ass like none other. Hos would get real jealous when they go out with Pat because she can shake a tail feather better than some strippers. But all in all she was still a dude. She could pull more niggas than a little bit with her chestnut eyes and soft pink lips. Her weave was undetectable and she would shake it as if she was born with it. Her friends would laugh because she still had a penis and they knew she couldn't play that off.

As Pat opened the door a cloud of smoke preceded her. She could see the disturbed look on my face. Pat just yanked me into the apartment and locked the door behind me. She walked behind me and asked me...

"Wassup girlfriend, what's going on?" as she puffed on her blunt.

Cheryl Sutherland

"Shit, girl that motherfucker is at my place, just standing there, as if he can see through my door."

"What the hell do he want girl." Pat said screwing her face up.

"I don't know. How did he even find out that I stay there?" I said looking puzzled.

"Well, you did all that you could but you know Tilak still loves you and he gonna find you sooner or later. He ain't going nowhere, fa' sho'!"

"Girl pass me the blunt. Shit I know, and that's the sad part. I got a date tonight so go up there and distract him. Let him know I went out of town or something, huh, here goes my keys. Tell him I gave them to you to water my plants while I was gone."

"Okay I'll do it just for you ... and to see how fine Tilak has gotten, then I'm gonna come back and rub it in your face for leaving him alone." Pat said.

"Shut up P." I yelled at her.

"Don't smoke up all my weed either." Pat snapped.

"Don't nobody want this bullshit ass weed girl!"

"I bet." Pat said as she snapped her fingers and walked off.

Chocolate Ty

Pat walked out the door and skipped up the stairs, she paused a minute when she saw him. He turned around when he heard the footsteps. Pat waved and walked by him and right to the door. She pulled out the keys and unlocked the door. Pat walked in and tried to close the door as Tilak walked in right behind her and asked Pat, "Where your homegirl at ?"

He looked around the apartment. Pat walked away as if she didn't hear him and hesitantly answered, "She went out of town, I thought you knew."

"How the fuck am I supposed to know her where-a-bouts. You know she don't talk to me no more."

"Well, she gave me her keys to water her plants while she's gone so that's what I'm doing. Do you have a problem with that?" Pat said trying to flirt.

"Yes I do," he said balling up his fist, "My problem is that she would let you know everything and not even speak two words to me. Three months have gone by and I haven't heard shit from her. I heard she was pregnant and lost my baby."

"NO!" Pat turned with her finger pointing in his face, "You took that baby from her; you beat her like she wasn't shit." Pat tried to hold back her emotions as she continued. "You acting like she wasn't your woman for the past four years. Tilak, You beat her like she stole something from you, like she was a perfect stranger."

Pat meant every word that was coming out of her mouth. She turned to walk away and water the plants as Tilak continued to question her.

"So you said she went out of town huh." Tilak said as if he didn't give a damn about what Pat just expressed to him.

"Yeah" Pat said with an attitude.

"Why you lying for her, Pat?" Tilak asked, "Now I know she's here. I just saw her give some punk-ass jit her phone number across the street. Now..." he said walking closer to Pat's face, "where the fuck is she?"

"Boy I just told you she out of t..." before Pat could finish her statement she caught one right on the left side of her mandible. Pat looked at him and started to tell him the truth but he just punched her again and again until she hit the floor. Then he took out his 9mm and began to pistol whip her. Blood splattered on the apartment floor. Pat started choking and screaming at him. He put the pistol in her mouth and yelled at her to shut up. He slapped her with the gun once again. He didn't hear a sound come out her mouth and her body didn't move. He placed his finger under her nose and felt air come out.

I could hear all the commotion from downstairs. I raced up the stairs almost tripping myself trying to run so fast. I made it to the apartment's opened door and saw Tilak standing over my friend, and Pat just lied there motionless. I went inside closing the door behind me and ran over to Pat's body and grabbed her. Pat's face was so distorted and bloody. Even some of her teeth were lying on the floor. I started crying and looked at Tilak and asked him why he did this.

He looked at me with a blank face and said "Did what?" while moving the gun behind him and putting it in the back of his pants.

I stood up and walked over to him and said "You a fucking punk. How many women you got to beat down before you feel like a man? Do you wanna whoop my ass again so you can feel even better?"

Tilak couldn't hear anything she was saying, her mouth was moving but no sound registered in his brain, all he could do was stare at her while tilting his head slowly from side to side. He hadn't seen that beautiful face in three months and all he wanted to do was fuck. All he could think of was her on his dick, riding it like she used to. The facial expressions she made when she reached ecstasy made his dick get hard. He then grabbed her by her waist and slung her over his shoulders. Blood started racing to his penis as he stepped over Pat's lifeless body. Ty tried to wiggle herself away from him but couldn't and just started balling hysterically. He tossed her on the bed and grabbed her throat with his right hand and undid his pants with the left. He was pressing so hard against Ty's windpipe that she couldn't breathe. As she started getting lightheaded all she could do is think about a way to get out of this. She knew her life couldn't end like this, with him trying to get his last nut. Tilak pulled out his penis and looked Ty in her face; he kissed her passionately on the mouth, as if they were going to make love. He tried to penetrate her but she was so dry. He knew he had to eat the goods in order to make it nice and moist, so he let her go. She gasped for air and tried to get up. He pulled the 9mm out of his back pocket and put it to her head and told her to lie down. She did. "Crraaaccckkkk!!" all she could feel was the cold metal hit her across her temple. She just shook a little bit and closed her eyes. Now Tilak could do whatever he wanted without worrying about her fighting, crying and trying to escape.

Tilak pulled off her sweatpants and thong and began to lick her clitoris and suck on her pussy until it was soaking wet. The taste of her juices drove him crazy. He thought about the shorty she lost and wanted to put one back in her and with that thought he thrust his manhood inside of her. He maneuvered slowly as if Ty was up and enjoying every minute of it. In his mind he was making love to her. He closed his eyes and imagined better days between them and how happy they were. He plunged back and forth inside of her until he came. She felt so good, his juices were inside of her and he felt the warmth of her walls around his penis once again. He sat there for a minute and looked at her. The frustration of being without her made him furious. So he figured that he wasn't done yet. He then flipped her over and put it in her anus. She moaned as she tried to regain conciseness and that turned him on even more because he knew she was alive and he could still get this pussy again. He pummeled her ass until it started to bleed. A whole foot of USDA beef all in her ass… and he loved it. He came so quick that he couldn't believe what he was doing. He skeeted his juices all over her so that when she woke up she knew it wouldn't have been a dream. He took off the rest of her clothes and left her there exposed. He decided that it was time to leave. He walked over Pat's body laying in the living room. He shook his head. He then pulled out his 9mm and shot Pat in the head. "The bitch never should've lied. One less bitch I got to go through to get to my baby" he said as he turned and exited the apartment.

I woke up a couple of hours later because of the continued vibration of my cell phone going off. I attempted to get up but the pain in my head made me lay right back down. I stretched across the bed to get my cell phone off the nightstand. I looked at the screen and saw 12 missed calls most of them were from my other friend Cheryl, a couple were from Vint and one from my mother. I never really talked to my mom ever since my mom kicked me out at the age of 17 for another man.

My mom was a man chaser. My mom never had her own; she always depended on a man one way or another. I would've understood that situation more if my mom was on drugs or if she was abused or anything like that but no, my mom just loved men. She went from one man to the next. It was just a continuous cycle. I thought back to Jeff, the man who gave my mom the ultimatum of choosing me or him, and she chose him.

I snapped back and thought about Tilak and how I've been with this nigga for four years and how he kept doing me like this. He just always found a way to do me wrong. I began to cry and look for something to put on. My phone went off again.

"HELLO!" I said in a very aggressive voice while putting on the sweatpants I had on earlier.

"Damn baby you just gon' stand a nigga up like dat." Vint said.

"Who the hell is this!" I said knowing who it was all along.

"This Vint baby. Damn, wassup, what da beat is, we still on for tonight."

"Uh? No…." I said trying not to sound to rude. "I had an altercation with Tilak and I need to get the police involved."

"You need me to come over?" Vint asked trying to sound concerned.

"Right now sweetheart, I really don't care what you do." I said hanging up the phone.

I put my jacket on and got up to walk into the living room to get some water and that's when I saw my friend lifeless body and her brains splattered on the living room floor. I lost it; I must have cried so hard and loud that everyone in the apartment complex had to hear me. I couldn't believe this but I had to regain my composure. I took a deep breath and stared at Pat for about another minute reliving our good times. I then said a silent prayer for her and called 911.

Cheryl Sutherland

I put a sheet over my friend out of respect. I felt my body going numb, I couldn't cry anymore, I couldn't swallow, hell, I could barely walk. I got my water and went to the bathroom and got four aspirins and sat outside on the steps and waited for the police to come. There was dried up blood on my face and in my hair, my ass was hurting so much that I had to lean on one cheek and rest on the stairwell's wall. I sat there staring at nothing, like I was in a zone. Then I heard footsteps ... it was Vint.

He looked down at me and asked me what happened and I just broke down crying in his arms. He just held me and told me that it would be okay. I disagreed with him telling him what I remembered in between me panting and trying to catch my breath. He stood me up and walked me towards the apartment as the nosey neighbors began to gather outside of their apartments. He got to the apartment door that I said was mine. He opened the door and saw the sheet on the floor with a noticeable body imprint underneath. He saw the blood and looked at me. I continued telling him the WHOLE story of my life with Tilak.

My biography was interrupted by a knock at the door. Vint asked who it was. The police officer identified himself and Vint told him to come in. It was Officer Bullard, he looked at me and looked at the sheet that covered the body on the floor and radioed for an ambulance, M.E. and coroner. He walked up to the couple and asked what happened as I looked up I felt a little bit of relief when I saw that familiar face. I then blurted out everything that I could remember to Officer Bullard. He tried to make sense of it all as he made a report of what happened then questioned Vint.

Vint told him that he just arrived two minutes before they got there. They all heard the sirens and soon after my house was flooded with paramedics, people from the medical examiner's office and the coroners. A paramedic cleaned my injured temple and bandaged it up. I then thanked them as they tried to encourage me to go to the hospital. I just got up in a zombie like state and walked to the bathroom. I started the shower and decided that this was all a dream until I took off my pants and saw some blood. I started to cry again. I grabbed the Cucumber Melon body wash from Bath and Body Works and let my mind drift into another world.

The shower was so hot you could see the steam coming from under the door. The police were trying to wrap things up when I exited the bathroom and walked into the bedroom to lotion my body with the Cucumber Melon body lotion. I took my time especially around my butt because it was a little tender.

I threw on a custom made Gucci sweat suit with a pair of matching Gucci Chuck Taylor sneakers. I giggled to myself when I thought about myself living in the hood and got a Lexus in the parking lot and some of the flyest gear in "The Raw".

I grew up for the most part in Riviera Beach, Florida. When I moved in with Tilak he lived in Royal Palm off of Forest Hill Road in an elegant gated community, until he put me in my own apartment. I came up real good when I was with him. Hell, life was great, I didn't even finish school in school, all I did was shop at the Wellington Mall, go down to Miami and shop, go to the outlets in Orlando and shop then come home and study with a private tutor. I was driving ever since I was 15 and got my license when I was 16 along with a beat up, hand-me-down car that barely worked, from my moms. When I met Tilak and he immediately got me into a 1998 Mercedes-Benz. I knew that he was the love of my life. I loved him, I loved that car, but each birthday I had to trade-in whatever I had into his cousins' dealership and purchase something more up to date. I snapped out of reminiscing and walked out of the room and grabbed my purse and cell phone.

─────────────── Chocolate Ty ───────────────

"Are we done here?" I asked Officer Bullard, "Am I free to leave?"

"Of course but there's one last question I need to ask you."

I listened as the officer asked me if the culprit had sex with me before, during, or after the attack and if I had any idea of who that person was. I acted as if I couldn't recall. I turned and looked at Vint and asked him if he was ready to go. He nodded his head. I turned and gave the officer a look to tell him that it was deeper than what he was looking at.

CHAPTER 4

I walked out the door with Vint, hand in hand. As we walked down the stairwell my mind was in a thousand and one places at the same time. My mind was scrambled until the warmth of this strangers palm brought me down. Even though I tried I still could not get my thoughts together until he escorted me to his 1977 Chevy Malibu SS.

I instantly fell in love with his car. It had an oriental blue paint job with white leather seats, white carpets with blue trimming. Leather Gucci convertible top and it sat on all chrome 24-inch Giovanna Lido rims. I got a little turned on once I saw how well he maintained his vehicle. "Just by his car I could tell he was a hustler. Not necessarily drugs but he had to sell something." I reassured myself.

We rode to the other side of town. Vint had the music blasting so every time that we passed by someone they had no choice but to look around and see what all the commotion is about. Just so the public can get a better view I asked Vint if he can put the top down. He asked me if my tracks were secure enough to blow in the Florida wind.

"Uh... yeah" I said sarcastically as we both laughed at his two-cent humor.

Vint put the top down and I enjoyed the breeze lifting my spirit. Soon after we pulled up to a stop light, I asked him to pull over to the Texaco at the corner of Blue Heron and Military Trail. I got out and went into the store to grab a 6-pack of Heineken and a package of Backwoods. I was so ready to get lit and take my mind off of the troubles that I was going through.

I jumped back in the car and Vint made a right turn onto Military Trail and made a left into a gated community called Woodbine. He drove through and turned in on Via Jardin Road. He pulled into a two-car garage home and jumped out. I sat there confused thinking to myself, "I thought he said he stayed off of Old Dixie and 2nd Street." I shook it off and got out of the car.

Vint brought me in through the garage entrance door that lead straight into his stainless steel kitchen with the breakfast bar, granite counter tops, steel bar stools, he even had wall murals. He grabbed my hand seeing that I was in amazement.

He led me to the all white living room with the genuine Natuzzi leather sectional, a custom 60" plasma television with Sony surround sound theatre speakers; he even had a white bear skin rug thrown in front of his ceramic fireplace. "A bear skin rug and a fireplace? As if he's not living in Florida", I giggled to myself. You could tell he didn't have any kids because the white leather was actually white. I took my shoes off and placed my neatly pedicured toes into the bear skin rug. Then I laid my tired and weary body on it. Before you knew it I was a goner.

My sleep was unsettling with the thoughts of what just happened to me and my homegirl shortly before this angel came to my rescue. All I could see in my dreams was Tilak's face with that evil ass grin. I used to adore his smile and sense of humor. I couldn't believe that he was everything to me and then shows me how the devil can operate. I was so wound up that my dream became a nightmare. The sight of seeing my friend brains on my floor replayed over again in my head.

I was awoken by the sent of purple haze in the air. I jumped up in a cold sweat. I could barely catch my breath. I looked around to see where I was at just to see Vint there, sitting on a stool, smiling at me, telling me how peaceful I looked sleeping so he didn't bother to wake me up. I thanked him and looked around for a clock just to see that I had been sleeping for an hour and a half. I walked over to Vint to ask him if I can take a puff of what he got and he handed me my own blunt that he rolled for me out of the Backwoods I bought earlier. I grinned so hard like I just won a prize and looking into his dark brown, comforting eyes, I felt like I did.

CHAPTER 5

Things progressed quickly between Vint and I. I was so comfortable around him. Between the police investigation and the funeral for Pat it seemed like months rolled by when it was only weeks. I was in a slump for the most part but Vint managed to keep me smiling. He even had a grin on my face when they put my homegirl under the earth.

Things just seemed so much more at ease when I was with him. He would take me out to the movies, 5-star restaurants and show me the more beautiful things in life and about life. He spoiled me just like Tilak did when I was with him. The only difference was that I didn't have to prove my worthiness to Vint, he just accepted me as I was.

All of this seemed too good to be true, from moonlit strolls on the beach to waking up in his arms every morning. He would do it all from massaging my body to playing in my hair, all I could do was think to myself, "Is this the *REAL* life of a thug, I never heard of a nigga brushing a bitch's hair before?"

After a month of Vint keeping me happy he asked me to move in with him. I barely stayed at my apartment anyways since the incident. I just got clothes and chilled with Vint 24/7. When he proposed that I move in with him I thought what the hell but I had to get some straightening first.

"Baby", I asked with a nosey demeanor in my voice, "remember when we met at the corner store."

"Yeah. Why?" Vint asked.

"You told me that you stayed off of 2nd street and Old Dixie, now is this your place or 2nd street?"

"Why, does it matter? I mean do you wanna stay out there." Vint said.

"No, that's not it; I just wanna know why you lied to me."

"I didn't lie to you, I do stay off Second Street when I am conducting business or at least that's what I want people to think. I mean would you really want a bitch or nigga to know where you actually rest your head when you in the type of business I'm in."

"True."

"I'm gonna tell you like this. I really dig you and all but I prefer if you don't get to deep in my business. The less you know the safer you are.

Understand." Vint said whole heartedly.

"Yeah, I understand."

So that was that. I didn't mention anything else about his other house. Hell I figured it like this, what I don't know won't hurt me.

I went upstairs to watch TV since one of Vint's homeboys came by the house. I decided to get out of their business and mind mine. In the midst of watching one of my favorite television show *Girlfriends* I dozed off. Sleeping in the upstairs master bedroom was like paradise to me until I heard yelling and all kinds of commotion going on downstairs. I thought it was all a dream until the noise became unbearable.

I ran downstairs to see what was going on. To my surprise it was a nigga trying to explain how a deal went wrong and how he's sorry and that he'll make up the lost money. My boo, Vint, wasn't trying to hear that and neither was his homeboy Flick. To me they were some O.G.'s for real. There's no explanation or story to convince them from not whoopin' yo ass. If your money was short so was a limb or a digit. Every time the stranger would come out his mouth the wrong way he would catch one in the jaw, temple or anywhere with Flick's .38. I never heard Vint raise his voice one time, so it was evident that Flick was the livewire, making all that noise along with the other nigga pleading for his life. Vint finally put a halt to things when he saw me on the staircase.

"Hold it down my nigga." he whispered to Flick.

"Why, Wassup?"

"You disrespecting my home 'cause you woke up my ol' lady."

"Sorry, stick (homeboy)."

"Yeah", Vint said walking up to me. He kissed me in my mouth as Flick stood there and the other guy whimpered, "I'm going to need you to go back to bed so we can finish some business".

"Okay", I said "But what's going on, are you going to explain this to me later?" He then glared at me as I turned around to say something else but he just placed his finger over his lips and waved me off like a four year old child.

As I lay in the king-sized bed and listened, there was nothing but silence. I wrapped up in the down comforter and I heard nothing. No more yelling, no whimpering, no pleading for lives, no commotion.

Nothing....just dead silence.

I woke up that morning to find Vint sleeping next to me looking so peaceful. I thought to myself what kind of business deal could've gone so wrong and all of a sudden ended up in total silence. Maybe Vint just dismissed it all. But I knew that was a lie. I know what he is into. I've been through this shit before but do I want to go through it again? I stared at him for a while before I kissed him on the forehead. I began to run my fingers over his pot belly to his manhood. Vint grabbed my hand, which startled me. He asked me if I was sure of what I was doing. I said yes and sealed the deal with a kiss.

    I straddled on top of him, grinding my pelvis around to stimulate his muscle. I began to kiss him on his neck and work my way down to his chest. I licked around each nipple which kind of tickled him. I moved down a little further to his navel. I played with his penis for a little while my tongue made circles around his bellybutton. I used my hand to measure his penis. Once I realized that it was just my size I took a deep breath and went for the gusto.

    All I could think about was making him feel good. I sucked his dick until it started to turn me on. He moaned a little bit that's when I knew whatever spot I hit I had to continue. I sucked him up and when I touched his genitals he damn near jumped out his skin. Vint started moaning for me to stop but I knew he wanted some more so I sucked my cheeks in and started sliding my mouth up and down his shaft like it was my pussy riding his dick.

Cheryl Sutherland

He grabbed my head and helped me slob on his knob.

The experience was crazy. I always had to get on my knees while I sucked Tilak's dick but with Vint it was more feelings involved as if he was showing me that I was making him happy. He pulled my head up and off his penis and told me to get on. I obeyed him and jumped on. I bounced up and down and then he grabbed my hips and put me in a rhythm that I didn't even know I had. He pulled me in closer to him, so close that it felt like he was in my stomach. I had to let out a moan when he was hitting something I never knew existed. He began to wind his body to the rhythm of mine.

I could've died. I felt the first nut coming but I wanted to keep going. It was like we interlocked with each other. Our bodies were made for each other. He then smacked me on my ass and told me to tell him when I'm cumming. I told him that I was about to nut and he picked me up off him and placed me on my hands and knees. I knew what was coming next the famous "doggy-style" position. That shit wasn't really so hot for me but I could pretend to enjoy it. But it was to my surprise when he penetrated my pussy with his tongue. I almost fell face-first into the pillows. I yelled his name out while he motioned his tongue like a vibrator against my clit. I tried to straighten my back so I wouldn't cum on his nose and mouth but he would place his hand right in the middle of my back so I could arch it for him. My thighs were shaking and my toes were curled so tight that I couldn't feel them anymore.

He paused and said "Let me know when you finna cum okay?"

I shook my head in agreement.

He then put his penis into my vagina and his finger in my anus and that was it, I yelled for God and told Vint that I was cumming he began to pound my pussy with such force I couldn't do anything but hold on. It felt as if my life was being drained out of me. My mouth was dry, my heart was beating so hard I knew I was going to explode. Then 3-2-1 he pulled out and skeeted his warm sperm all over my ass and my back. I collapsed onto the bed and he was right behind me. He whispered in my ear "Good morning."

CHAPTER 6

A couple of months flew by and I was getting pretty bored. We were together all the time. We were living together, sleeping together, eating together and riding around town together everyday. I had my own whip and everything but every time I wanted to go somewhere or do something by myself he would offer to take me or keep me company. The only thing that I felt that I could do by myself was take a shit.

So I came up with a bright idea and I suggested to my baby that I get a job. He asked me if I was sure that that's what I wanted to do. Me being me I assured him that was my choice. He said his stickman Big Al owned a club down on Okeechobee Boulevard and he had a position open for a bartender if I wanted to do that. He knew Alfred since he was little and he called him his stickman because he stuck with him through thick and thin.

I agreed to work there because I love the club

scene and I knew that I could get all the tips. He called Big Al up and told him what the beat was and Big Al told him to bring me there at 4 o' clock.

Vint tried to give me the rundown on Big Al and how he was his stickman and all but first and foremost he was a MAN. So if he tried any thing with me to let him know off rip so there won't be no static. When we pulled up to the plaza I had a puzzled look on my face.

"Vint, what is this shit, this look lame baby." I said.

Vint looked at me all cock-eyed and exclaimed, "What! You never been to Club T.K.O. before? Man this is the hottest shit in Palm Beach County. The club is owned by a famous boxer but my man Big Al manages this shit and makes sure everything is tight."

I was overwhelmed by the enthusiasm in his voice I had to bust out laughing.

"Damn bay, I hope you getting a cut too the way you blowin' up his spot." he just giggled and jumped out his Chevy Avalanche.

Big Al greeted him at the door and gave him a big hug and they slapped five's as Vint introduced me to Big Al as his girlfriend. He said not to rub elbows with me too tough 'cause I am his, and he gets very jealous about me.

Chocolate Ty

Big Al laughed and joked on Vint 'cause Vint never had a "girlfriend" he just had hos and tricks and don't forget about the bitches either. In the midst of their joking and reminiscing I walked up to Big Al and extended my hand for a handshake. He looked me up and down and told Vint he now knew why I'm his girl.

As he examined me, I observed him. He was a big dude like he played football. He was very sexy and he knew it. I smiled as he escorted me into the club. It was huge, I mean huge. It had a performance stage, a V.I.P. lounge area, a separate room just to take pictures, 3 bars and 2 dance floors. It was very nice. I felt embarrassed about the remarks I made about the club minuets earlier and Vint knew it 'cause he just looked at me and gave me that smirk. My reaction to the club was like none other, it was as if I belonged there. Big Al then took me and Vint to the V.I.P. lounge area and showed me the tricks and trade of my position as a bartender. He pulled out a list and asked me some questions.

"Have you ever bartended before?"

"No."

"Do you know how to fix a simple drink as in vodka and cranberry or Hennessey and coke?"

"Yes, I can do that."

"Can you keep tabs on money?"

"You mean can I count money?"

"No, I mean can you keep tabs on it because in this business money goes in and out of registers just as fast as you can blink. People ask to make change and you need to know who took what and how much."

"Oh yeah, I can definitely do that."

"Well then you're hired. I'm going to tell you how to make it in this business." I drew myself deeper into him as he unlocked the door of making money. "The secret is," he continued, "that you have to out-do everyone else. You have to make the bomb ass drinks without using too much liquor. You have to keep your hair done, your dress code gotta be G, you need to smell good, your makeup need to be flawless I mean that's if you wear any. Nails neatly manicured. Men love a well kept woman and if you have the attention of men then you get the majority of customers, ya dig? So all in all keep your mind on your money and money on your mind. Oh yeah one more thing," Big Al added, "Don't let my register come up short."

It took me a moment to absorb everything he just told me. It was as if he wanted me to prosper in this business. I leaned over to give Vint a kiss on the cheek and felt Big Al eyes on my round plump ass.

Chocolate Ty

Big Al then made the remark "Damn nigga I see why you sprung".

Vint replied, "Damn right, you'd be sprung too if you had her. But you don't, so the next time I catch you checking her out…"

Big Al quickly cut him off and blurted, "Hey I can look at what ever my eyes lay upon."

To calm them down I thanked Big Al once again and asked him when my first night was. He turned around and told me Friday night. That's three days to get my shit together. I agreed with Big Al and turned to Vint and grabbed his arm. We both walked out the door as I leaned over to ask Vint if Big Al was always so "to-the-point".

Vint just said that Big Al is 'bout his business, a very lucrative and prosperous one at that.

We walked over to the truck quietly. I could tell Vint was upset. Vint walked me to the passenger side of the truck and opened my door for me. He smacked me on the ass and I turned around and gave him a smile to let him know that it was alright. He closed my door and hopped in on his side. He leaned over and kissed me. I told him he better stop before I rape him in his own shit. We both laughed as he suggested we go down to City Place to get something to eat.

Now City Place is a plethora of restaurants,

clubs and boutiques. It's always packed so if you out cheating on your significant other City Place is not for you.

When we reached our destination we walked around for a little bit and finally decided to go to a place called Wet Willie's, which is a comedy club, bar and restaurant in one. We sat at a table and ordered two Call-A-Cabs, a frozen drink mixed with alcoholic.

Vint and I drank our frozen drinks. It's funny because the alcohol never gets to you until you're on your second drink. Vint ordered our next round and I went to the bathroom to touch up my make up. When I walked back out, I saw some chick sitting in my chair. I walked up to Vint and slapped him in the back of his head.

"Get up' now!" I insisted. The girl got out of the chair and stepped back looking at me all crazy.

"Excuse me sister girl but you don't know me. I'll fuck you up bout putting your hands on him."

"Well I suggest that you do what the fuck you got to do 'cause regardless if you wanna fight or not this is my man and it's gonna stay that way." I said stepping closer towards her.

Vint just sat back smiling. All guys enjoy the entertainment of girls going at it about them.

"Vint you better get this girl, I don't want to

have to fuck her up before she meet momma." she smiled and said.

"Damn baby this is my sister" he replied.

I felt so stupid. "Oh my god I am so sorry," I said apologetically.

"That's okay, Vint I'll see you later and call momma sometimes," the girl said walking off.

"Vint baby I'm sorry. You know I get very jealous about you." I said as I busted out laughing.

"Yeah, ha-ha," Vint said sarcastically. "Girl you got some heavy hands I started to turn around and rush you but figured it couldn't be any one else but you." he joked. But my smile turned stiff as my eyes locked on Tilak walking through the door with the same girl that I caught him with at his house.

Vint looked at me and asked what's up. I just raised my hand and pointed to Tilak. He looked to where I was pointing at and asked who it was. I just blurted out, "Tilak!"

Tilak turned around and locked eyes with me. He gritted his teeth and the chick just grabbed his arm tighter.

Vint grabbed me by the waist and told me to come on. He dropped fifty dollars on the table and took my hand. My feet were shuffling against the floor. I couldn't take my eyes off of him. I just yelled at him, "You Bastard!"

Cheryl Sutherland

The whole lobby fell silent.

Vint just put his head down.

Tilak looked at me as if I was cheating on him. He started to walk towards me but the girl grabbed him and told him to leave me alone. He snatched away from her and steadily came towards me. I was standing there, adrenaline rushing as if I knew we were going to fight. But for some reason I wasn't scared. I don't know if it was because Vint was there or not but when he approached me I stepped right up to him. There we were chest to chest. I didn't see or hear anyone or anything else. I was face to face with the demon of my life and I wanted to rebuke him. I hated him so much that I wished that he would just drop dead. At that instant Vint stepped in front of me and asked him if there was a problem.

Tilak answered him very abruptly. "Jit, this don't concern you." and tried to move Vint out of the way.

"First of all, this does concern me because this is MY woman. So whatever took place when she was on your team it's over, 'cause it's my turn now. So let's just leave civilly and that's that."

"Shut the fuck up! Bitch ass nigga! What you too weak to defend your woman. Shit when she was mine I would put a nigga to sleep 'bout her. I guess you don't like her that much. Huh, I don't blame you she done let herself go anyway." Tilak said looking me up and down.

He was lying; he knew that I was fine as fuck. He just was hot 'cause I was with somebody else. From the look in his eyes I knew that he wanted to tear fire from my ass but there wasn't anything that he could do, we were in a public place and I had my boo with me. I wanted him to try something so that Vint and I could jump his dog ass.

Vint then turned around and looked at me as if he was analyzing what Tilak just said. In the blink of an eye he turned around and with all his might he caught Tilak with a left hook. He knocked Tilak clean off the floor and then Vint rushed him in mid air. He jumped on top of him and kept hitting his head into the floor. I saw Tilak eyes roll to the back of his head.

I started to smile.

The chick he was with tried to get Vint off of Tilak but he was a beast. He pushed her big ass down to the floor and all. I yelled out to him- because I was not going to put my hands on him- and that's when he stopped. He stood up and walked off, just as the bouncers were coming and left me behind. It was like he was in a trance. I had to power-walk to catch up with him. When he reached the elevator I had to jump in with him.

I tried to kiss him to show him my appreciation of what he just did for me but he avoided my kiss. There was nothing said and definitely nothing that I could do to make him look at me. We just got into the truck and drove off. It must have been the quietest we've ever been around each other. I think that was the longest ride home ever.

We pulled into the garage. He just got out of the truck and slammed the door. So I jumped out.

"What are you supposed to be mad at? Me? Or are you just ignoring me for fun?" I asked.

"Ay yo, Ty, just kill the noise right now. I just damn near beat a man unconscious with my bare hands. Ty I damn near killed him and didn't feel no way about it."

I never thought about it from his side. He could've gone to jail over me. He can still go to jail if Tilak press charges. Evil doesn't die easy so I know Tilak will be okay.

That night I held Vint in my arms until he fell asleep. I rubbed his head and back just to ease his tension. I was worried that maybe this episode pushed him over the edge. I thought about what just happened and just smiled to myself and eventually nodded off to sleep.

Chocolate Ty

Vint woke up in the middle of the night. He just stared at Tyrena because she just looked so innocent and peaceful. As she slept he thought to himself, "Am I falling in love with this girl? That was not an option. It wasn't part of the plan. But the shit I've done for this girl is more than I've done for any woman in my life…shit this ain't going right for me. It's okay she put me in a dangerous situation before and I was cool wit that. Now let's see if she gonna be my ride or die bitch." Vint laid back down and held her. Ty felt his grip and woke up to ask Vint what was wrong but he just kept mumbling to himself that he was sorry over and over again.

CHAPTER 7

Today's the big day! I start my job at the club. I feel so alive and brand new as if I have a purpose in life. Vint still has been acting funny since the incident with Tilak, he's been so quiet and he don't even get riled up to have sex with me. Whatever his problem is I know he better get over it, I thought to myself.

I walked to the bathroom to start my shower. It was 2:30 and I had to be at the club by 4:00 so Sarah could show me how to fix the drinks. I started to take my clothes off when Vint came in the bathroom.

"Can I join you?" Vint asked.

"Of course, baby." I replied.

He seductively took off the rest my clothes, slapped me on the ass and instructed me to get in the shower. He then began to take off his clothes. He walked over and got a washcloth and went in the drawer to get the body wash. He pulled the shower curtain back and got in. He lathered the washcloth and began to bathe me. He glided his way from my breasts to my back. He kissed my neck and started down my back kissing each vertebra on the way down. He got to my ass and kissed each cheek. He took his fingers and ran them from my stomach to my clit. He then inserted his fingers into my mound.

He knew it was something that I yearned for, that feeling of being wanted, being desired. Something he has held back from me for three days. He knew I adored what he was doing. He could tell that I was loving each moment by my facial expressions. He slowly pulled his fingers out and turned me around. He got on his knees he gave me a hug and rested is head on my stomach. He lifted my leg and rested it on the side of the shower's stall. He gently kissed my sweet spot. I grabbed his head as he began to work his magic.

I loved when he went down on me. I knew that we were meant to be. I know that I was being contradicting when I thought this but no other man on earth could ever make me feel this good. I was caught up in what he was doing until my explosion of lust interrupted. Vint then picked me up and leaned me against the wall. He put his key in my ignition and started to make love to me. I came in like two seconds. My bottom lip was trembling and I tried to call his name but no words would come out. His dick was rock hard. I knew he was going until he came so I just held on for the ride. Vint steadied his pace as he lifted and lowered my body to the beat that was in his head. I felt his manhood inside of me. It felt like we were having sex for the first time. My hair was getting wet and I didn't care. I just wanted this second nut. His rhythm began to pick up pace until he was beating it in.

It felt so good.

"Vint, baby, uh oh, you freakin' me" I managed to get out.

"I know baby I'm just making up for lost time" Vint boasted.

"Keep doing what you doing baby" I urged him. I felt the second nut about to cum. Vint grabbed me by my throat and that made me come off rip. He pumped about two more times and came inside of me. All I could think about as he loosened his grip was... this is love. He rinsed off and walked out the shower. I took the washcloth and continued to bathe. I was so weak but I was so happy.

I got out the shower and looked at Vint lying on the bed naked and sleeping. You know that's good sex when you go right to sleep, I giggled to myself. I closed the bathroom door so I could play my music and blow dry and wrap my hair. I put in my Juvenile cd "400 Degreez", and played my song, *'Flossin' Season*. The song began to play and I started to vibe with it. I pulled open the drawer that held my flat irons and noticed a long gold box. "Game tight take a tramp make her out a champ..." I sang along with the track while deciding if I should open the box, "It's all gravy playboy 'cause it's flossin' season..." I continued to sing.

I weighed my options, this was my house and me being me... and that's being nosey, I opened it. I screamed at the top of my lungs. It was the most beautiful thing I ever saw. A tennis bracelet; it was 14k gold with 1.5 t.c.w. of diamonds.

"CMR Millionaires let 'em know it's flossin' season everywhere!" I yelled out imitating Lil' Wayne's verse. Vint came in the bathroom. I looked over at him and he had that smirk on his face.

"Baby is this for me?" I asked.

"Oh you just finding that..." he replied.

"I love it!" I said hugging his neck and giving him a kiss on the cheek.

"I hope you'll feel the same way about me one day," he said as he turned and walked off.

I had a blank look on my face as I thought to myself on how he came to my rescue at the apartment after only knowing me for a hot minute.

I knew I couldn't let him go. I continued to dry my hair. I wrapped it and tied a satin scarf around my head. I went into the walk-in closet and tried to find something to wear. Everything I had I felt as if it wasn't sexy enough for the mood I was in.

"Ay girl!" Vint called to me.

"Hmm?" I answered.

"Look under the bed."

I bent over to see what he was talking about and there it was a garment box from Chanel. I yanked it from under the bed and pulled it out of the box. I laid the outfit on the bed and just stared at it; a black and silver Chanel cat suit that accented every curve that I had. It was as sexy and beautiful as I felt at that particular moment.

I ran in the closet to find my black Chanel open-toed shoes. I hurried and lotion my body with the sweet smell of Peony from Bath and Body Works. I got a thong out of my vanity drawer and put them on. I walked back to the bed and picked up my outfit and brought it back to the bathroom with me.

When I got into the bathroom I put my outfit on, shoes and all. I took my wrap down and flat ironed the hell out of my hair. I got out my make-up bag from M.A.C. and put on some eye shadow and my M.A.C. Viva Glam IV lip glass. That's it. I am the perfection of beauty. Seductively, I walked out of the bathroom and into the bedroom.

"Do you like what you see mister, grrr?" I asked trying to portray Eartha Kit.

"I like that little outfit. I think I did a good job picking it out." Vint said. "Your bracelet would set that shit off though." he added.

"I know..." I said as I pulled my arm from behind my back.

"BLING, BLING!" we both said together in a roar of laughter.

Vint got up and walked to the closet to put on some basketball shorts. I asked him if he was going to take me to the club. He shook his head in disagreement.

"Drive your truck and shine on them hos," Vint suggested. "And if you need me call me."

CHAPTER 8

I pulled up to the club in my Lexus truck a little nervous but anxious to get this money. When I stepped out my truck I knew that it should've been a red carpet awaiting my feet 'cause all the females were staring me down, they could've at least put some toilet tissue on the ground since I was the shit.

Everyone was waiting for Big Al to come and open the club. All the security guards were trying to holla but I kept telling them that I was taken. Big Al rolled up in his Navigator truck with the big 26' Sprewell rims. He maneuvered himself out the truck and walked up towards all of us. He said that we were going to have a meeting today about appearances as he glanced in my direction. He walked towards the double doors to let us all in. We all walked into the V.I.P. lounge and took seats. Big Al walked behind the bar and started his speech.

To my surprise Big Al used me as an example

of what he wanted to see in the club from now on. I am very confident in myself because I have class, elegance and beauty but I knew I made enemies after that but I didn't care. I was in it for the money. When he started to get too expressive about what he wanted and using me as his example, I had to discreetly let him know he was crossing the line.

Sarah took me over to our bar to see what I remembered about what she showed me about bartending. I mixed a couple of drinks and she showed me how to make the most requested drinks. If somebody wanted something that I didn't know how to make then I should just let her know. Sarah was very quiet and to herself. I made sure to use her only when I needed her.

The club opened at 8 o'clock for the social crowd. They just threw in a Jazz and R&B mixed CD and let it play. This was more of a laid back crowd. You know the people who worked the office jobs and just needed a drink to unwind. It was slow but I learned a lot; everyone had a story to tell from investment bankers to real estate agents. They taught me a few things and they probably didn't even know it. I just poured and mixed drinks and listened to their problems, their solutions, their recommendations and in return I collected my tips.

Four hours has passed and it was now

Chocolate Ty

midnight. The social crowd was dying down and the rowdier crowd was piling in. I made over three hundred dollars in tips and about 15 business cards with little notes of them telling me to *"call them"*, from the social crowd, so I knew that I can make a stack before the night is over with if I got these niggas drunk enough. I was uneasy keeping my money in the tip jar since it was mostly twenties and tens, so I would just empty the larger bills in my purse and keep the dollars in the jar. About 1 a.m. I sent Vint a text message to come and make a pick up. He returned my text by saying that he'll call when he get there.

    Vint pulled up about a quarter after 2 a.m. and at that time I had over seven-hundred dollars in my possession. He called my phone and I signaled to Sarah that I was going to the restroom. She just waved me off.

    I walked to the back door of the club to meet Vint. While walking back there I was thinking on how I can make three hundred more dollars before the night was over, but I knew that I could come up with it. It looked like Vint was glad to see me in one piece.

    "I just knew that they were gonna work yo' ass in there, but you look good, as if you ain't even sweatin' it."

―――――――― Cheryl Sutherland ――――――――

"I'm not, I'm taking everything slowly and at my own pace. I think them girls in there are jealous of me 'cause Big Al used me as a example of *"HOW-TO-BE-IN-A-NIGHT-CLUB"*. I joked.

"I could've figured that, but anyways what you got for me."

"Seven right now but I'm trying to get a stack before I go home."

"I heard that shit. Well hit me up when the club let out."

I handed him the money gave him a kiss and walked away. I felt very uncomfortable when I walked back in. It was as if everyone knew what I just did. The night was winding down. It was a little after four in the morning and I was tired. I made another three hundred and eighty-six dollars before the night was out. I helped Sarah clean the bar then went into the bathroom to fix my makeup. I fixed my self up and went into a stall to use the restroom. That's when I heard the two bitches that will make my job a living hell...Trina and Carmen. The two most broke down hos in Palm Beach County.

They been working at different bars for the last five years and ain't did shit for themselves. They share a one bedroom apartment downtown. Got a beat up, old ass '92 Honda Accord that they share between them and all them damn kids they got.

Chocolate Ty

These hos ain't shit.

"I hope that bitch don't think she all that. Her stupid ass, the only reason she probably here is because she fucked Al."

"I know Trina; you ain't speaking nothin' but the truth. Everyone done been through that and I know that ho ain't no different. Soon as she see dem dolla signs that she think he throwin' at her, she's going to get caught up until the next female run through here."

"Carmen, I got a trick for that bitch. She in here sucking up all the tips and shit. Flirting with all the niggas and acting like she friends with all the bitches that come through here. I will expose here true colors."

At that moment I flushed and came out the stall. I gave each one a glare to let them know that I heard every single word that they said out of their cock sucking mouths. They don't even know me to be up in my business like that. I walked to the sink where they were standing. "Excuse me" I said. All they could give me was an "umph". I washed my hands while they giggled amongst themselves and walked out the bathroom. To think about it they probably did that shit intentionally. While they were walking out Sarah was walking in.

"Wassup girl."

"Nothing much." I sighed.

"Ty, you can't sit there and tell me that lie when I'm looking at your face and can tell something's wrong. Oh yeah I wanted to apologize about earlier. I get very frustrated when I'm at the bar."

"Oh, I just thought you disliked me too."

"What are you talking bout?"

"Yeah, I just overheard Trina and Carmen talking about me. They think I'm fucking Big Al. I got this job because of an interview I…"

"I know you not letting them hos get you upset with their dirty asses. Them hos talk about everybody that's better than them. Anyone who looks better, talk better, smell better, shit if you fuck or suck better they gon' have something to say. Fuck them. So what they talk about you, and… who gives a fuck."

"I know, I know."

"Well if you know get yours and leave them in the dust working at this shit hole. I only work here because Big Al's my husband and instead of hiring someone to work in my spot he wanna keep me here. I know them bitches fucked my husband and they phony ass going to speak and keep speaking as long as Al's the co-owner of this shit. It just shows me how hos really work."

Chocolate Ty

"Damn, are you serious?"

"I sure am. But Al told me about you and Vint. You know they go way back. Vint a silent partner in this club too. I really hope you know what you're getting' into with that one. He's very sneaky and controlling. I'm not being a "Hater" but he is Al's ace. So keep your eyes open. Don't be a fool."

On that note we both left out the bathroom and walked towards the front entrance. I told her I'll see her tomorrow and I walked into the V.I.P. lounge and tried to call Vint. He didn't answer his cell phone or the house phone. The thoughts of Vint being unfaithful started racing through my head. I tried to keep myself as calm as I could while I raced towards my truck. The security guard tried to walk me out the door but when I saw Trina all in Vint face by my truck I picked up the pace even more. Vint had a look on his face as if he was aggravated by Trina but he didn't want to loose his cool. When he looked up and saw me he met me half way and gave me a big hug and slobbed me down. I saw her cutting her eyes at me. But I knew that trick was still gonna try to get mines.

"Where is your truck?" I asked while wiping the excess saliva from around my mouth.

"I had my home boy drop me off so I could ride home with you. Why?"

Cheryl Sutherland

"Oh nothing I just wanted to know," I enquired. "What homeboy dropped you off?"

"You don't know him." He said bluntly.

"OK."

Once again our drive home was very awkward, very silent. When we pulled up to the house, he jumped in his truck and told me he'd be back, he had to go to his house on 2nd street.

"You don't want me to come with you?" I questioned him.

"Naw I'm straight. Go get some rest. You had a tiring night. When I get back I hope you rested because I want some of that sweet punaney when I get back."

And he pulled off.

I smiled and walked into the house.

CHAPTER 9

Vint pulled up to 2nd street and parked in front of the house. He waited until a car pulled up next to him. He rolled the window down just enough to release some of the purple haze smoke that was about to choke him.

"Wassup, jit. How's it hanging?"

"Shit, I just got back from the club with Ty. You straight from the other night."

"Yeah I'm good. I thought you were starting to get serious with a nigga or something."

"Naw, I just had to make that shit look real, that's all. Sorry though."

"Come on nephew you straight. You know I'm hard-headed anyways. So do you think that she recognizes anything yet?"

"Hell naw. I think she's falling for me though." Vint said.

"Oh, the bracelet and outfit I bought her, is going to make her feelings go up a notch with you.

That's the only reason why she was with me so long. But I got some money for you. You can give it to her so she can go shopping tomorrow. Take her to the outlets in Orlando. I'm gonna run into you there so make sure that she's in a good mood so she don't make a scene."

"I got you unk (uncle). But what if she don't want to go?"

"Regardless, call me and let me know where she gonna be at and I'll visit her there personally."

"So, when you gonna go check her at the club?"

"Soon jit, soon." At that time Tilak gave Vint a brown bag with five grand in it. Tilak hesitated on the next question he had to ask.

"You got me on that bust next week?" Tilak inquired.

"You bet unk. We done cased da joint and all. We just need them thangs and it's a deal done," Vint replied.

Tilak sized Vint to make sure that he wasn't going to mess up his money. He's been casing this guy for months now. Making sure that all the jewels this nigga owns, all the money this man got stashed in his house all came back to him. The drugs were a bonus, if they found any. Tilak had to make sure that it was going to go down, the right way.

Chocolate Ty

"Make sure you let that money I gave you last for the week. So at least you'll be covered until you hit that lick (robbery). Give her a couple of hundreds here and a grand there okay."

"I got you unk."

"Aight jit."

They both pulled off. Vint felt like an asshole for doing this to a girl he actually liked. He knew that in the 'hood your word is your bond but he knew that he was taking it too far. He thought about the consequences if Ty found out. How would she react? Would she even believe him if he told her his side of the story?

Well, in all aspiration, he hoped for the best. No matter what, blood IS thicker than water.

CHAPTER 10

I woke up to the sound of Vint's phone going off.

"Baby get that!"

"Man," Vint mumbled "Fuck that phone."

"Then turn it off! It's been going off all morning." I answered him in a not so pleasant tone of voice.

Vint sat up and looked at me like I was crazy. He reached over and turned the phone off. I got up and reached for my phone to call my homegirl Cheryl. I haven't talked to her since Pat's funeral. It was about ten in the morning on a Saturday and I know she's at the mall. I pressed the number 4 and the <TALK> button on my phone because she's on speed dial.

"Yo."

"Wassup girl where you at?"

"The mall." Cheryl said with an attitude.

"Wassup, what's wrong?"

Cheryl Sutherland

"Nothing I'm just wondering why you calling me. What did somebody else die that we know?"

"Girl it ain't like that. I just been busy. You know trying to come up. Come on don't be mad at ya girl."

"Why should I be mad at you? You got Vint in your life, I ain't got shit, nobody but my money."

"Where's Terrance?" I asked.

"Hell if I know, but when you do see him, let him know that I was pregnant."

"What you mean was?"

"Just like I said, *WAS*. I got an abortion on Monday. I told his simple ass that I was pregnant Sunday before last and he left and never came back."

"What?"

"Damn, You hard of hearing."

"No, I'm shocked. Cheryl you love kids."

"I know but I'm not gonna raise my child by myself. You can't help me. My mom's stay too far away to help and I refuse to do it on my own. Fuck proving a point. This nigga left me because I was pregnant. All these years, all the hos I done whooped over him, all the weed and crack I stuffed up my pussy for this nigga and he going to leave me? This is the time when I needed you Ty and all you can do is think about yourself. Fuck, Ty I needed you."

"I'm coming to where you at. I swear I'll make

it up to you. What mall you at?"

"Wellington."

"Well I'm going to jump in the shower and I'm on the way."

"Umm-hmm."

After I hung up I told Vint what the plan for my day was. He told me that he wanted to take me to Orlando to go shopping. I told him that Cheryl needed me and I was going to her. I asked him for the money I gave him last night. He got up and went into the pants he had on last night. He pulled out a fat ass stack of money. I knew that wasn't the seven hundred I gave him last night.

"Where did that come from?" I asked.

"It's from the run I made last night." he quickly answered.

"Oh, well can I get a stack, please," I begged.

"Here," he said with his arm stretched out.

"Thank you," I grinned.

I jumped in the shower and took a PTA shower (that's when you wash your pussy, titties, and ass). I was in and out in about 4 minutes. I ran to the closet and pulled out a red Dickies dress with matching sneakers. I pulled my hair back into a ponytail. Picked the money up off the bed and gave Vint a kiss. I stuffed the money in my Dickies purse as I raced down the stairs.

Cheryl Sutherland

"Tyrena!" Vint managed to yell.

"What Vint?!! I gotta go!" I snapped back.

"Come get your cell phone. I gotta call you don't I or you don't wanna be bothered wit' me today?" he said thinking about if she ran into Tilak.

"Sorry, I forgot" I replied as I ran back up the stairs and into the bedroom to get my phone and left out again.

It took me 40 minutes to get to the mall. I called Cheryl to find out what store she was in. Of course she was in Macy's, her favorite store in the whole mall. People knew her by name especially at the M.A.C. counter. I met up with her inside the mall. She looked great. She had on a Fendi skirt outfit with matching sneakers. I got my style of dress from her and her other friend, Shavon.

Shavon was a girl she met when she moved up to Virginia to get away from Terrance. I think at that time they had broken up for about 4 months. He drove all the way up there to get her. She brought Shavon back with her to give her a taste of Florida. Shavon was real cool, a rebel in her own way.

Shavon and Cheryl were the exact same height; Shavon was very bright skinned, with shoulder length auburn hair, she had a stocky yet slender build and the sexiest legs that you could imagine. She had a tongue ring that she loved to play with while talking to people. Shavon used niggas like toilet tissue; she would use them and throw them away.

She could get whatever she wanted from them without even fucking them. The words that came out of her mouth were like candy and them niggas just ate it up. She had niggas head over heels 'bout her before they even knew her last name.

Cheryl called my name before I could see where she was. She has the eye of an eagle, that's why Terrance stayed getting caught up 'cause Cheryl could spot him from a mile away. I ran up to her and gave her a hug. She said she wanted to go to the car to put her bags up and then walk through the mall. I agreed and helped her carry her bags. As we walked through the doors I dropped a bag of clothes. An outfit for a dude fell out.

"I thought you didn't know where Terrance was at?" I asked her.

"I don't and that ain't for him."

"Then who is it for?"

"It's for Flick."

My mouth dropped. "Flick who?!"

"Yo, Flick bitch, Vint homeboy."

"Oh, hell naw! Girl, why you ain't tell me."

"Because I haven't spoken to you until today."

I looked around in disbelief.

"Damn, then why his ugly ass didn't tell me. He be at the house everyday. Eating up our food and sleeping all in a bitch's house. What the fuck type of shit is that." I laughed.

Cheryl and I caught up on the things we've missed out on. We promised to call each other everyday and not let this twelve year old friendship go to waste.

CHAPTER 11

Vint rolled around in bed. He really couldn't sleep that well when Ty's not next to him. He turned his phone back on and saw the envelope on the screen which indicated that someone left a message. He knew who it was from and what they wanted. He went to the house phone and called Flick.

"What up, dog? Damn turn your radio down. It's early in the morning and you with that bullshit. Man, I'm just calling to see if you ready for today?"

"Yeah, I'm right round your way," Flick said with the music still blasting. "What y'all got to eat?"

"Ty ain't here, she gone to meet her home girl Cheryl at the mall. She didn't cook anything before she left either," Vint said.

"Did you say Cheryl? I hooked up wit her the other day. I got that bitch sprung, She at the mall shopping for me!"

─────────────── Cheryl Sutherland ───────────────

"You think you a pimp, don't you? Man bring yo' ass on so we can hit this lick and gone bout our business."

"Be there in a minute."

"Bet."

Vint went into the bathroom to take a shower. He always let the water run for a minute before he gets in. While the water runs Vint goes to the bed and pray before he showers, he pray for forgiveness for the sins he has committed and for the sins that he's about to commit. He knows that he's no saint but as long as he repents he feels as if he can walk with his head lifted.

Vint took a shower and walked into his closet with his towel wrapped around him. He heard the downstairs alarm motion detector go off which indicated that Flick had arrived. He looked around for what outfit to wear for the day. He picked out a Beige ENYCE outfit that he bought from New York Men's Clothing with some Timberlands. He sat on the edge of the bed and pulled out a black garbage bag. He took a deep breath as he looked inside and counted his guns, two glock 9's, a .25, two .38's, and he knew that he kept his Desert Eagle in the kitchen drawer so yep, they were all there.

He got dressed and galloped down the stairs. He saw his homeboy sitting in the love seat with a disturbed look on his face.

"What up, boy!" he said excitedly.

Flick just stared at him then looked at the staircase. Vint got to the bottom of the staircase when a stranger tried to take his head off with a bat. Vint ducked and snatched the bat away from the guy so fast that the guy fell over. Dude was dressed in all black with a mask on. Vint placed the bat in the middle of the guy's chest and started to press down slowly. Vint felt the cracking of the outsider's breast bones. He applied more pressure as Flick stood up and walked towards the front door. He turned and looked at Vint to signal that there were two of them and one of them had a gun. Vint didn't give a fuck; this guy had violated the sanctity of his home. What if Ty was there, what if he didn't have a quick reflex or wasn't fast paced?

His emotions went into a rage.

"Fuck nigga, who sent you!!" Vint demanded.

The stranger didn't say a word. Vint had a solution for the stranger's quietness. It didn't matter what face was behind the mask he was gonna kill them. Vint leaned over and took his mask off. It was a teenage boy. Vint shook his head and signaled Flick to come over there. Flick walked over and asked Vint what he wanted him to do. Just at that moment the other stranger ran from by the door.

Cheryl Sutherland

Flick tried to run after him but Vint told him to forget about it because they had who they needed...the one with heart, not the coward.

"Grab the big trash bags from out of the pantry. We gonna have to put this youngin' to sleep. I don't give a fuck who you are now because from this point on you no longer exist."

Vint grabbed his gun from behind his back and stuck it in the boys' mouth. A tear rolled down the teenager's face.

"Naw nigga don't cry now, you big enough to try to take my head off but you ain't big enough to die for what you believe in, for what you work for, for who you are or who you working for. Shit, that's the definition of being "Gangsta" you gotta live and breathe that shit young one and guess what? These are some of the repercussions of what you do lil' nigga this ain't television boy, this ain't BET or the movies, this real life faggot!"

Vint was yelling so much that he was foaming out of the mouth. Vint took a step back with the gun still pointing at the juvenile; Vint wiped the corners of his mouth and told Flick to come on. Flick grabbed some twine rope and Vint grabbed the boy by the neck, the boy tried to fight Vint off while they tied him up and placed tape over his mouth. He wanted to tell Vint what he wanted to hear but Vint wasn't trying to hear it.

"Lil' nigga you had your chance, you determined your own fate and here it is, life's a bitch and then you die." Vint was so serious about what he was saying.

Flick didn't even say a word because he knew that would fire Vint right back up again. They dragged the minor to the basement. Vint was silent the whole time as they took the boy to his final destination, that's when Flick knew that he was gonna kill the little boy. That's what he did that morning when that nigga came up short with his money. See, Vint wasn't a confrontational person because he knew that he could loose his cool in a heartbeat. Vint just didn't want any one to think that he was a push over. He was a cool cat and didn't really bother anyone. His only friend was Flick and now his girl Ty.

Now he had to kill this guy because he had to send that message. A message that needs to be sent to most young one's..."You can't fuck with an O.G." Just as soon as they got him in the basement they placed the kid's head in one of the trash bags, Vint pulled out his nine and blew the kid brains out...without the blink of an eye.

They cleaned up their mess and put the boy in the cargo of Vint's truck. They drove out to Lake

────────── **Cheryl Sutherland** ──────────

Worth and they put him in a dumpster. They made a quick stop to change into there "Bust Boy" gear...black on black. They had to head out to Boynton Beach for that lick they had to do. They went by one of Flick's girls house and got her unregistered 1989 Ford escort.

They got to the spot but there were cars parked in the driveway. Flick didn't care. He put a silencer on his .38, got out the car and went right to the front door. He knocked on the door. A little girl opened the door and he snatched her up placing his hand over her mouth and put the gun to her head. She tried to scream out but couldn't. He walked into the house unmasked and armed. Vint jumped out with his mask on and firearms ready. Flick walked around the house. He walked into a room where there were two ladies sitting and talking. She yelled out for the little girl. Soon as the little girl didn't respond she got up to look for her but found trouble instead.

"What are you doing in my house!" she screamed.

"Shut the fuck up and lay the fuck down! Now, who else here?" Flick whispered.

"Nobody", the lady said hesitantly while lowering herself to the floor.

The other girl sat there dumbfounded. She

also got onto the floor. Flick let the little girl go and told her to lie down also. She was crying but obeyed his orders.

Vint walked past the room and saw all the people on the floor. He went straight for the money room. He walked in and the nigga was sitting right there counting his stacks. Before he could get up and ask Vint anything, Vint shot him right between the eyes. Flick heard the gunshot and looked at the lady who lied and said that no one else was there. He put the gun right to her temple as she pled for her life. He shook his head and put her in the same place that her man was at. He killed the other girl and the little girl.

He walked up to room that Vint was in. He saw dude laid out and Vint getting that paper. He helped Vint grab everything in sight, money, drugs, they took the jewelry off the guy and the chicks and all the money out of his pockets. They ransacked the whole house in record time. They ran back to the car and sped off. In the midst of fourteen minutes, Vint and Flick made seventy-six thousand in cash, about eight grand in jewels and another twenty-four thousand in drugs.

Job well done, or so they felt, one thing that hey had to remember was *KARMA*.

CHAPTER 12

I didn't feel like going to work tonight but I knew that I had to go. I was in a very shitty mood. This working at the club shit was getting old quick and there was something on my mind that I just couldn't shake. I barley spoke to Vint and I just didn't feel like being bothered. I went into the bathroom to analyze myself. I stood naked in the mirror to see if I could look into my soul. I ran my hands over my milk chocolate skin. I was trying to sculpt a new me in my mind. I began to cry because there was an obstacle in my life that I had to get over…Tilak.

It seems as if he's on my mind everyday. It seems like everything reminded me of him. All the way down to Vint. His lifestyle and the way he treats me. I felt as if we are meant to be together. I turned on the shower and just let the water beat on me, massaging my worries and doubts down the drain. I got out and put on a robe. I let my body unwind on the bed and dozed off.

I woke up to Vint talking on his cell phone in the room. He was engaged in a conversation with Flick. I pretended as if I was still sleeping.

"Wassup, dude? What's poppin' for the day?" Vint asked.

"Nothing that I know of homie," Flick replied.

"Well I need to get up with you, if you know what I mean. I know that shit kind of dry round here but we at the top of the ladder. If our supplier got locked up we need to find other resources."

"I know a dude up in VA. He holds major weight. His prices aight too. If you want I can give him a call and see what's good."

Vint rubbed his chin in thought, "Yeah holla at ya boy up north then let me know what's up."

Vint hung up the phone and jumped in the bed.

"Bay, you sleep?"

"Umm hmm", I answered him.

"You go to work tonight don't you?" he asked.

"Yes I do Vint. Didn't I just tell you I was sleeping?" I hesitantly said "Why, what's up?"

Vint looked me up and down and licked his lips "You need a ride or you straight?"

I jumped up because I knew he was up to something.

"Vint, cut the bullshit what do you want?" I

was angry at this time 'cause I already knew what he was getting to but I was not going on a run with him. He knew he struck a nerve so he rose up out the bed.

"I was gonna ask you if you wanted to go on a lil' vacation but that's okay." he said with his head down as if I really hurt his feelings. I knew he was playing around but I just joined him.

"Oh, I'm sorry baby. You know I'm cranky when I wake up from my naps. I would love to take that ride with you." I was lying through my teeth but I had to make it believable. "But you know I just started working at the club and I need to make that money. So why don't you go and I'll hold the fort down." I felt as if he got the point.

"You don't like road trips huh?" he asked.

"Nope." I replied with a big grin on my face. He just laughed at me and had that damn smirk on his face. I could tell that he was up to something.

"Wassup baby? Do you really need something from me or is that all you wanted to ask me?" I inquired.

"Yeah matter of fact I need to get rid of the rest of this dope. Do you mind slanging it at the club? You already can make up to a G a night but you can triple that if you do this for me."

"How the hell am I supposed to do that Vint?"

Cheryl Sutherland

"Just ask them if they smoke and if they say yes then ask them "clean or dirty" if they say dirty or if they say they "smoke woo" then hit them up with the dime bag of soft but add it on to the price. You selling a nic' bag for the price of a dime bag and a dime bag of white then that's twenty bucks in your pocket. It's enough niggas at the club for you to make a cool grip in one night. I'm not going to be here so make sure you keep yo' shit tight and carry that .25 with you."

"I didn't even agree to this shit yet but I'll do it. Just because I'm your bitch and don't you forget it."

"I won't baby, I got you…always and forever." as he sealed that comment with a kiss.

I raced to get to the club tonight because I wanted to see what these hos had to say tonight with their raggedy asses. I felt as if I was THE SHIT tonight I was working this Fendi pant suit I got from Cheryl as a birthday gift last year. I wore it with no bra or shirt under the jacket and some black knee high Fendi boots with the pants tucked in the boots. The boots were simple it just had the Fendi symbol on it but it brought out the outfit.

The night went by really fast. Before I knew it I had over sixteen hundred in my purse. I was slanging yayo, weed, X- pills and all, as if it came standard with the drinks. I had my game tight. This was the beat right here, this is definitely what the people wanted. I would rap to these niggas as if I knew what the fuck I was talking about but hey, if they bit I kept serving. I told Big Al that I wanted to leave early. He said if I could get Trina or Carmen to take my spot then I could leave. Now that was fucked up, he knew that I didn't get down with them like that and I knew that he didn't want me to ask them hos shit and get messy in his club. I swallowed my pride and walked to the bar downstairs. I looked at Trina first.

"I need to know if one of you can work my bar so I can leave?" I reluctantly asked. Trina and Carmen both looked at each other and laughed.

"What's your problem? Why do you need to go? You trying to catch Vint in the act or something?" Trina said with her BMW (body made wrong). I looked at them as if looks could kill.

"You know what, don't worry about it." I said and turned and walked away. "Y'all too ignorant anyways" I added.

"WHAT?" Carmen big-nosed ass yelled out. "What you got to say?" I walked back and got right in Carmen's face. I wanted to spell it out for her so I talked real slowly and harsh.

"I said that you two are some ignorant

bitches." I said pointing at them. Carmen started with the name calling and so-called telling me about myself. I looked at Trina and she just stood there grinning. Then I walked away. I sent a text to Vint to tell him that I couldn't get off early to see him off.

I went back to my bar and Sarah asked me what all the fuss was about. I told her it was nothing and not to worry. She told me to keep my eyes open for them hos I just had a conversation with.

It was about 2:45 and the club was going to let out in an hour or so. I was tired and that's been going on a lot lately and I don't even know why but I'm always so tired.

"Excuse me can I have a Hennessy and Coke?" I looked up and it was Vint.

"Hey babe," I said leaning over the bar to give him a kiss since public affection was one thing that Vint was big on.

"I got your text so I decided to come up here. I'm gonna have to go though or do you want me to wait on you?"

"Yeah, you might need to 'cause them bitches got beef with me and some shit might go down." I said keeping an eye on them.

Vint told me he was going to inform Big Al about what happened but he still was gonna have to leave before the club let out. I agreed. I handed him the money that I had on me and he gave me a kiss and then he disappeared into the crowd. I got a text a minute later saying that he was gone and to take care.

The club was so packed, everybody was vibing and feeling good. The DJ played one of Triple J's new song and that's when I started feeling uneasy and shortly after I figured out why. Tilak came up to me and ordered a drink.

"Hennessey and coke." I hurried, got that drink together and I slammed it on the bar.
"Is that all?" I asked.

"No. I want you too." He said with an evil grin on his face.

"Tilak, on some real shit you need to get out my face before I make that phone call and you get your ass whooped again."

I was enraged. Who gave him the authority to even say something like that to me?

"Listen to me, bitch. If you only knew the half you wouldn't be over there selling out, you stupid ass little girl."

A red flag came up but of course I ignored it.

"How bout this, pay for your drink and get the fuck out my face."

I stared him down. WHOOSH! The next thing I knew I was wearing his drink. I was stunned and embarrassed. In all the confusion I forgot about the tricks that had beef with me. I got some napkins and wiped my face. I looked around and Trina wasn't at her bar and Tilak was gone.

I took everything in stride. I cleaned up the bar so fast as soon as the club let out. I called Vint on my cell and told him what happened. He empathized with me and all but didn't make a u-turn to come to my rescue. He stayed on the phone with me so I can feel secure. But I fell silent in horror as I walked to my truck. All four of my tires were gone, rims and all. All my windows were busted out. Someone had keyed it and everything. My truck was ruined.

Vint was steady calling my name but I could not respond to him. He hesitated for a minute and finally said fuck it and got off I-95 and asked me where I was at. I finally told him at the club still. He said that he was on his way. I said okay. I walked in circles to think of what to do. At that point Big Al, Sarah and two of the bodyguards walked out.

"What the hell happened to your ride?" Big Al asked.

"Trina did this to my shit" I said.

"Well do you need a ride?" Sarah asked.

"Naw, Vint on the way."

"Are you sure?" Big Al asked one more time.

"Yeah I'm gonna call the police and make a report." I assured him.

I watched them walk away and pull out of the parking lot. I started to cry. I called the police and sat on the curb. I looked at my cell phone and it was 4:07 a.m. I had my head down deep in thought of who really would've done this to me. Tilak or Trina? As I pondered in thought I heard some footsteps behind me. I knew it was Vint. Then I noticed his shoes. Vint don't wear those type of shoes. I hurried to look up and it was that familiar stranger. He greeted me with a blow to the head.

CHAPTER 13

  I woke up blindfolded, lying on my side on the cold tiles. I felt the cold air on my body so I knew that I was naked. I figured that I was not outdoors or in an abandoned building because of that fact. My body was sore. It felt like I was punched and beaten for an extended period of time.

  All I could do was think of a way out. I knew that I was a dead woman if I didn't. I was gagged and bound. I thought I was by myself until I tried to yell out. At that point I got kicked in my side and was told to shut up. I whimpered as I heard his voice. I knew that I was going to die. All I could do is pray. Tilak knew that I would tell if he let me go.

  He sat me up in a chair. He kept rubbing on my breasts and touching my vagina. He kissed me in my mouth and told me to tell him that I love him. When I didn't he told me to say goodbye to Jit 'cause this would be my last day on earth. I thought to myself. Who the hell is Jit? Then I thought back to the incident at the restaurant when he called Vint a jit then. Then I thought back to the times when we were together and he always call or get a phone call from a guy named Jit. He never used a real name. He just always said jit.

    Now I was furious. I know the hell these bastards didn't set my ass up. It couldn't have been like that. I love Vint and I know he loves me. I just broke down and started crying some more. I tried to talk but all my words were slurred and muffled. At that point Tilak took off my gag and asked me what I was trying to say because he would love to hear it.

    I responded to him in a hypothetical way. "What do you want from me? I haven't done any thing to you. What? Do you want me back? I'll be with you. I swear Tilak." he slapped me across my face.

    "Shut up, you dumb ass bitch, I hate you! You lost my baby and you made my life hell. I told you that I couldn't be a day without you. I keep tabs on you Ty, see Vint, he worked for me. I hired him to be with you. See I was gonna let Jit use you till I was ready for it to stop, but I know that he's catching feelings for you. So I have to get you two apart before he ruins everything for us. It was all a set up, you meeting Vint at the store, the money, the house, the fight at the spot downtown even the lifestyle you were living. When I say everything I mean EVERYTHING!" I could tell Tilak was beyond being serious about what he was saying.

"Us? Who the fuck is us?" I managed to get out with my jaw hurting.

"Me and you bitch. You know that we were gonna get back together one way or the other. Vint was just a rebound. He was gonna break your heart and I was gonna rescue you. But Vint, that sorry motherfucker, couldn't keep his end of the bargain. So off with your head." he laughed.

"Off with my head?" I thought. "Tilak on some real shit. It ain't even worth it. Just let me go. Please baby." I knew I fucked up with that but hey, if I was gonna die, why not try. I heard Tilak footsteps get closer to me until I felt his breath against my face.

"I love you Ty." I heard the gun cock back. "But yo ass got to die. I can't live on this earth with the thoughts of another man lying next to you, feeling on you and making love to what was once mine. I believe in the saying, "If I can't have you no one can." I take that shit to heart. So now I'm going to take that in my hands. Today I'm GOD."

He put the cold steel to my temple. I just waited. I stopped crying. I stopped praying. I was just there. He pulled the trigger...<click>...nothing happened.

He started laughing.

I didn't respond.

"What, you too good for a joke? I see Vint done turned you into a soldier. You stopped crying and everything. What I'm supposed to let you go because you knuckled up. Man fuck you!" At that time he loaded the clip in the gun...POW! POW! POW!

He shot me three times. All I could do is try to steady my pace and try not to panic. In my mind I knew the injuries weren't serious. Or at least that's what I tried to convince myself. The wounds were burning and I was losing it inside but I couldn't show that to him. I just slumped my body in the chair.

Tilak ran over to me and whispered in my ear "Before you depart this blessed earth I want your last memory to be a fond one." he struggled to take off my blindfold. He held my head steady as I tried to focus. I was in my own shit. He was trying to kill me in my own house. He let go of my face and walked out.

I tried to fight for my life. I could see the bullet holes in my body but I still tried not to panic. I had a hole in my chest, my arm and my neck was stinging. I figured the bullet must have grazed my neck. The house phone began to ring. The answering machine picked up.

"Babe I can't find you, if you're home please pick up the phone. Pick up the phone Ty. I'm worried about you. Baby please. I got your truck towed to the house. I hope your there to sign for it. I'll talk to you later."

When I heard his voice I broke down. The nigga I was in love with set me up and have no regards about it. If he gets home before I bleed to death I got something for him.

Half an hour passed and it was now 4:40 in the morning and this dummy hasn't made it home yet nor has the tow truck came. I started to just let go and go on home to Jesus. I said a prayer to myself. I asked God to forgive me for all my sins but if he does spear my life I will forgive Vint for what he did. I'll even forgive Tilak but I won't forget. I just sat there and thought about all the things I could've done different in life. I could've went to college, I could've forgiven my mother for betraying me. Cheryl and I could've been better friends. I just let my mind go and let the Lord take over. It was all up to him.

I heard the beeping sound of the tow truck reversing. Then I heard knocking at the door. It was the tow truck guy. In my mind I was screaming for help but in reality it was just above a whisper. Then I heard him conversing with Vint. I guess they pulled up at the same time. I heard the keys jingling in the door. My heart got filled with so much joy. He walked in with the tow truck driver and when he saw me his expression was like none other.

"Oh my God! Ty are you okay?" he asked as he slowly approached me.

"Do you need me to call the cops, Vint?" the tow truck driver asked.

"Yes, please." Vint replied. He got on his knees and looked me in the eyes. He stood up and walked to the hall closet to get a sheet to cover me up. He then untied me and laid me on the floor. He saw that I was shot. "What the fuck?" he said as he examined each one. I didn't even flinch when he touched my wounds.

"Who did this to you baby? Answer me Ty. I swear to God I'll kill them. Who was it?" he asked as if he didn't know. I kept myself quiet because I knew that I was gonna get better and when I do he was gonna get it. Him and Tilak.

"The cops and an ambulance are on the way. They said don't touch her. Is she okay?" the stranger asked.

"Yeah man. I hope that they hurry up. I can't believe a nigga would disrespect my home. I hope you knew who did this to you 'cause I can't have this shit going down. Not like this, not with you

Chocolate Ty

Ty."

I just lay there, listening to him babble on. I just wanted to die to get away from all the bullshit that he was trying to spit. He knew who the fuck did this to me. I just had to close my eyes and let nature take its course but it wouldn't so I just pretended.

Damn, I wish this nigga would shut the fuck up, I thought to myself. He's the reason I'm in this mess and now he wanna care. My mind wondered until I heard the sound that put me at ease. *Oh there goes the sirens I'm in the clear. I'll just have to deal with this asshole another day. When I get the chance to regain my strength.*

"Ty, I love you. Be strong girl, be a soldier for me. Come baby fight it, fight it." Vint continued to say.

The paramedics came in and got me situated. They let Vint know to meet them at St. Mary's Hospital. They assured him that they were going to do any and everything that they could do to save my life but I had lost a lot of blood so they had to hurry. He agreed and said that he would be there.

CHAPTER 14

I hate hospitals but I definitely gotta get better.

I went through surgery fine and when I recovered Vint was right there by my side. All I did was think about how in the hell did I get myself into this mess. I really do love Vint but this is like the ultimate betrayal. I felt as if he knew that I knew something because when he's here I constantly looked at him and rolled my eyes. How is he going to explain this? He's been here every day for the last 2 days and hasn't explained shit. I'm bout to tell him that I know it all but I want to give him the chance to get it off his chest. I guess he think that I'm going to leave him. I can't....I don't have anywhere else to go.

Vint walked in the room and gave me a kiss.

"You feel better today?" he asked me.

"Yep." I answered.

"Do you know who did this to you?" Vint inquired.

"Yep." I said.

"Who?" he said while getting out of the bed. I flipped the subject and asked a question I had to know the answer to.

"Vint, do you love me?" He looked at me puzzled.

"What? Why would you ask me something like that?" he conjured to get out.

"Because I need to know, I don't want to continue a relationship with you if you don't love me," I let him know.

"To be honest baby, I do and I was trying to fight that feeling. I'm not used to this and I'm trying to get with it."

"Well would you lie to me, or cheat on me?" I inquired.

"No." he quickly replied.

"Then why did you set me up to loose my life." the words poured out of my mouth. He stepped back and looked at me. He gazed from the tubes and IV cords that hung from my body to the constant beeping of the monitors. He stared up at the ceiling then back at me. I just stared back at him.

"Well?" I asked him.

His eyes filled with tears as he inhaled and let out a deep sigh. He then turned and walked out the door. I yelled out his name but he didn't even

Chocolate Ty

pause, so I laid there and I just looked at him walk out the door. I started to pray that he would return.

"Lord I don't know why we only pray to you when we are in difficult situations. I sin everyday, I barely got to church, I never acknowledge your grace and presence on a daily basis or the fact that you allow me to live through the circumstances I face from day to day but I need you now more than ever. Here I am, I have a person that I love deeply and dearly but I'm not strong enough for him or to be with him. I need you to give me the strength to deal with him, to understand him. I want to be with him and I know that he is confused but I know that he cares for me. I know that you are a mighty God and a merciful God. Have mercy on me, have mercy on us. Lord God send him back to me in a way that I have never seen before. Full of love and full of honesty. In Jesus name. Amen."

I lay in that hospital bed with tears streaming out of the corners of my eyes. I waited with all the hope and premonition that he would come back. But he didn't. I just counted the hours as they went by.

The next day Cheryl came by the hospital. Of course she had some gifts. Two dozen roses with a heap of get well soon cards and balloons. I even had a card from my mother and her new boyfriend.

──────────────── **Cheryl Sutherland** ────────────────

Cheryl sat on the bed beside me and began to brush my hair.

"Sister Girl, you've been through a lot in your life and God's had your back the whole time. You know that God has a purpose intended for you so I want to know what are you gonna do with yourself."

"What do you mean? Am I gonna get saved or something." I said in a raspy voice.

"Not necessarily. I mean every step you take needs to be in faith. Just let the Lord be with you and acknowledge him as your savior."

"I've already done that. But let me ask you a question?" I suggested to Cheryl.

"Okay."

"Did you know anything about this?"

"About what Ty?"

"That Tilak set me up."

"Set you up? No. You telling me this whole thing was a set up?"

"Yes Cheryl. Tilak told me everything before he shot me. He told me how Vint was a set up, me meeting him at the store, the fight at Wet Willie's, the money, the lifestyle even my job at the club, well he didn't say the club but he might as well have because he said everything."

"What?!!!"

"Umm hmm. I asked Vint about it and he just

walked right on out the door. He hasn't called or came back since yesterday." I sobbed.

"Oh he done pulled a Terrance huh?"

We both laughed at her comment.

"I guess so. Damn Cheryl what am I gonna do?"

"Well do you love him?"

"That's the sad part about it, I do. I know he didn't set me up to get shot but he was wrong for being with me because Tilak quote, un-quote ordered him to."

"Yeah Ty, but do Vint love you."

At first I never would have thought about a question like that but I had to sit back and think about it this time. I always had a feeling that he loved me but now love was a feeling that I knew he didn't posses. Even though he sat right here in this spot and told me that he did, did he mean it?

"Cheryl on some real shit, I have no clue." I said.

"Well, we both knew that he was dead ass wrong for the stunt he pulled but he's a man. They don't know any better, no matter if the situation is big or small. I mean anything's okay, as long as it benefits them. You have to guide them and if you're lucky enough they will follow." Cheryl preached.

I turned to lie on my side. I really had to think

about this. I was in between a rock and a hard place. This nigga became my whole world in less than a year and now I find out some shit like this. What the hell am I gonna do?

"Cheryl you know what. Vint is my man and I'm not gonna let Tilak win. He's not gonna run me away from Vint. I know Tilak, and he would be more distraught if I stayed with Vint. Either way I win. I'm with the man who I love and who makes me happy, and the man who's given me hell won't like it at all." I satisfied myself in saying this because I felt as if it was the truth...or was it?

CHAPTER 15

Home doesn't feel the same since all this has happened to me.

It's sad that Vint wouldn't even pick me up from the hospital. I walked around the house and noticed some things were missing. The bear-skin rug was gone. I guess I must have bled on it. The couch was gone, we had a new one. A couple of our pictures were missing; I don't know what to say about that. I walked upstairs and Vint was sitting there on the corner of the bed reading a bible.

"Oh, so know you want to find a spiritual connection. You're reading the bible to figure out what to do next?" I said casually.

"Dang, hey baby." he responded.

"Hey." I said while I started to pack up my belongings. I didn't feel comfortable with him there. I really wanted to stay but I didn't want to impose or put him in danger.

―――――― Cheryl Sutherland ――――――

"Where are you going?"

I turned and looked at him in way that he knew I wasn't even playing.

"I know you didn't just ask me that stupid ass question. Does it matter where I'm going or even if I live to see tomorrow?"

"Yes, it does."

"Well I'm gonna go stay with Cheryl for a while." I lied. I had no where to go but a motel. "I see you don't want me around anymore. I asked you a question when I was in the hospital and yet have I gotten an answer."

"Bay," he said getting out of the bed "I didn't know how to answer your question. I didn't set you up for that to happen to you."

"Then what did you set me up for Vint?" I interrupted.

I could tell he was getting a little upset as well as ashamed. Ironically I didn't care but I did. In the back of my mind and in my heart I knew that he would not have let me get hurt if he was there. He would have protected me from it all.

"Tyrena, on everything I love. I will kill this nigga. Just say the word and he's dead. I promise."

"You would do that just because I asked you to."

"If that will make you stay, of course I will

baby."

 I looked at him and continued packing my bags. Vint snatched the bag away from me and dumped all my clothes out on the floor.

 "Did you hear what I just told you?"

 "Yes I did Vint."

 "Then why are you still packing. What, you really don't want to be with me?"

 "Vint it's not that I don't want to be with you, I just don't want you to get hurt. I don't know what the deal was between you and Tilak but obviously Tilak don't want us together. I'm cool wit' that and all but I want you to know…if you ever want to be with me you will have to show me your affection for me to believe you."

 "Damn a nigga just got paid to keep you around. I felt as if it was the best bargain in the world. I get to be with you and get paid for doing it. Ty you were the perfect girl when you was with Tilak. Your name ain't in the streets and shit. You a dime piece and you got your shit on lock. I tried to keep myself from doing the shit but he eventually talked me into it. This house, I paid for it, but Tilak furnished it. Half the shit in your closet was on the behalf of Tilak.

 "That nigga loves you for all the wrong reasons. I love you because you're real. You are a lady and you know how to carry yourself like a queen. On the days when I feel as if I'm not shit or worthy to be in your presence you remind me that that's all a lie. You make me feel good Ty, just when I'm around you. My days don't begin until I see your smile. Baby, don't walk out that door. I need you."

"At that point I knew that Vint and Tilak were related. They say the same corny ass shit," I thought to myself.

"Well we spent the last five days apart so two more won't hurt. I need some time to think."

"No. You're not leaving. You can't just leave." Vint demanded as he stood in the doorway.

"The fuck you mean I can't just leave! That's what the fuck you did when I was laid up in the hospital! How dare you say some shit like that to me. Not even a phone call. Not one phone call from the time you walked out on me at the hospital until now. Get the hell out my way. I'm gone!" I screamed.

At that point in time I was ready to walk away from it all. No clothes, no car and no where to go. But I was gonna get out of his presence right about now.

"Alright fine." he said as he moved to the side to let me by.

Now this was too easy, there was minimal fighting and yelling. I was a little sacred that as

Chocolate Ty

soon as I make it past him I was gonna catch one in the back of the head or he was gonna push me down the stairs...but nothing. He just let me go.

I started walking down the street. I picked up my cell phone to call Cheryl and asked her to give me a ride. She was cool with it but she disagreed about me leaving Vint. By the time I got to the end of the block I heard the music in Vint truck behind me. He rode along side me in all black. I stopped and asked him.

"Where are you going?" he looked at me with tears in his eyes.

"I'm about to go make a liar out of you."

"Excuse me?"

"Yeah, in the back of your head you think I'm lying. You think that I'm not a man of my word. Well if my own uncle made the woman I love leave me because of his ass then he got to go." he proclaimed.

I couldn't help but feel sorry for him. I stopped him in his tracks and got into the truck. I called Cheryl on her cell phone and told her never mind. When we got back to the house we had nothing to say to each other. Our eyes said it all. All it took was one kiss. I knew he meant what he said and I wanted it to go down that way. He took me in his arms and didn't want to let go. I swear that was the

———— Cheryl Sutherland ————

best sex I ever had.

CHAPTER 16

I woke up the next morning with Vint holding me very tight. I gave him a kiss on the cheek. I got up to use the bathroom. My stomach was cramping all night. I got to the bathroom and noticed that there was some blood in my underwear. I went to get a panty liner and started the shower. I stepped in and the blood flow began to get heavier. I yelled out to Vint and he came into the bathroom.

"What's wrong?"

I told him to look into the shower. He saw all the blood and began to panic.

"Fuck. You want me to call an ambulance?"

I nodded my head.

The pain was excruciating. It felt as if my intestines, liver, and uterus were going to come right on out with the blood. I began to squat down to help ease the pain. All I could do was think about when I lost Tilak's baby. I hope this is not the same scenario.

Cheryl Sutherland

Vint came back in and helped me out the shower. I threw on an old jogging suit and waited for the ambulance. I didn't want to sit on the brand new furniture. I had to change my pad twice before the ambulance came. When the ambulance did arrive I hopped in with them and Vint followed in his truck. When we arrived at the hospital I saw the same doctor that treated me for my gun shot wounds. He asked the paramedics what the problem was. They told him heavy vaginal bleeding. They admitted me to a room and Vint was by my side the whole time. They ran tests and found out that I was pregnant and had suffered a miscarriage.

All I could do is yell out "AGAIN!"

That was it! I began to cry hysterically. I was about to snap. Vint just held me and rubbed my arms and back. I felt his tears on my shoulder. It seemed as if we both wanted this unborn child and we didn't even know it.

After a while, Vint got up and called Cheryl. She was there in no time flat. I told her what happened and she felt for me. I had cried so much and so hard that my eyes were swollen. We sat quiet for a moment and then Vint said he was going to get us something to eat.

I knew Cheryl didn't have the answers to my questions but I needed to vent.

Chocolate Ty

"Why, Cheryl? Why me? Why do this stuff keep happening to me? I feel as if I'm going to snap. Go out of my mind. I don't understand what I'm doing wrong?" I said looking towards the ceiling. I prayed, "God I'm sorry for whatever I've done or whatever it is that I'm doing. Please just give me the strength."

Cheryl walked over to the window. She stared outside for a little while. She then turned around and preached, "Ty, I know you going through a lot right now but God never gives you more than you can handle. You're gonna make it through this with your pride and dignity. See Tilak just trying to break you down but you have me and Vint on your side. He's gonna have to break all of us down before he can win."

"I don't know if I can take any more. One of us is going to end up dead and right now death is knocking at my door."

"Don't talk like that. We won't let him do anything to hurt you anymore. Guaranteed, even if he has to loose his life about this."

She sat on the bed next to me. The hug she gave me was so comforting and sincere. That's the reason why I love her with all my heart and soul.

Vint walked back into the room with some sweet smelling Pollo Tropical. He knew that would cheer me up. We all ate in silence; we could just about tell what one another was thinking. But silent we remained.

Vint got finished eating his grilled chicken and yellow rice first and asked me, "Baby remember what I said, all I need is your word and it's done."

"I think I'm going to take you up on that offer," I replied.

"We both gonna handle that." Cheryl interjected. Vint looked at me as if Cheryl was joking but I gave him a head nod to let him know that she was serious.

"No, we all gonna handle this" I said "but we'll talk about this when we get to the house."

The doctors released me that next day. They gave me a prescription for some antibiotics and a pamphlet on how to cope with the loss of a child. I already knew how I was gonna cope with this problem.

CHAPTER 17

We arrived at the house and started to plot and scheme on how to take Tilak out of our lives for ever. I asked Vint if he was gonna let Flick in on the plan. Both he and Cheryl looked at me as if I was crazy.

"Sorry, my bad," I giggled.

Vint got up and rolled a couple of blunts. I got up to put Lauryn Hill's CD The Miseducation of Lauryn Hill in the CD player. We blazed up but this wasn't my regular purple.

"Vint, what's this baby?" I asked.

"It's Chocolate Tah." he answered.

I busted out laughing.

"Are you serious?"

"Yeah but you don't have to get jealous, you get me just as high." he said with that smirk I love so much on his face. At that point I knew we were going to be alright. When track three came on Cheryl and I were singing as if we wrote, produced and

Cheryl Sutherland

performed that song for a living. When the music is turned up loud enough we just know that we were the originators of that song.

An hour later we were all high.

Hell, we even paused on our plans of plotting against Tilak. We just sat back and chilled. Soon after, Vint and I were being very affectionate towards each other on the couch. Cheryl was sleeping. She can't handle the power of weed. I wanted to go upstairs and suck Vint up since we couldn't have sex. I whispered my request in his ear. Of course he accepted. We started to walk upstairs but were interrupted by knocking at the door.

Vint hurried to the kitchen to get his Desert Eagle .44 Magnum out of the drawer. He slowly walked to the door and looked out the side. I walked back down the stairs to see who it was. I went and sat on the couch that Cheryl was laying on. She was awoken by the knocking on the door also. We sat there as Vint held a conversation at the door. It was a woman. He stepped back and allowed her to come in.

My eyes got huge. I couldn't believe what I was seeing. If it wasn't already the worst week in my life this ho had to make it even worse. Yep it was the bitch I caught Tilak with at his house. I analyzed her from head to toe. She was fucked up.

Her hair was standing on top of her head. Her clothes were half ripped off her body. Her eye was black and blue but you could tell that was an old bruise. I already knew what happened to her. She didn't have to tell me her story but Vint had to ask.

"Damn Lisa, what happened to you?"

"Me and Tilak got into it." she whimpered while having a seat.

"Why, for what?"

"Well he's been acting funny for a while now. He started snorting powder and shit. He just been acting a fucking fool. I was putting up with is nasty ass habit but a week ago he came home acting real crazy. He said that he's cut off all the loose ends that were holding him back from me. I was okay with that and all but when I tried to leave to go home that night he flipped out on me. He started hitting me. He never ever put his hands on me before. We been messing around for all this time and just got serious over the past year and he has always been sweet to me."

She was saying that as if she was mad at me because what happened to her. I looked at her as if she lost her mind.

"What you trying to say? Are you blaming me for what happened to you?" I inquired.

"In a way it is your fault. You should've never

Cheryl Sutherland

fucked him up like that. He was gone off of you and ever since you had an abortion with his child he been acting crazy." she said.

"Excuse me. I didn't have an abortion. He whooped my ass just like he did yours and that's how I lost his child. You fucking dummy!" I was heated by that comment. How could Tilak lie like that? This bitch had to go I couldn't take anymore. So I stepped to her and said "I know you got to be used to this by now. Get your ass out my house!" Lisa looked at Vint and he just shrugged his shoulders.

"What you expect him to say stay bitch. GET OUT!" I said walking closer towards her. If I would have taken two more steps I would've been stepping on her toes.

Lisa stood up and looked me up and down. I never realized how tall she was until now. All I could do is think of a way to drop this Neanderthal if she tried to pull some tricky shit. Lisa took in a deep breath and looked me up and down one more time. Before I knew it I was getting slick with her again.

"Damn ho, do you see something you like? What, you want some of this pussy?"

Lisa laughed at my comment and retaliated by saying, "I might as well get some too since you sliding down the family's pole you trashy bitch!"

Chocolate Ty

she interjected.

I could not believe she said that to me. I wouldn't have been so mad if it wasn't true. But it was the honest to God truth.

Vint saw that the comment hurt me and started to walk towards me. He was yelling for Lisa to leave and telling Cheryl to get her out of here. But I didn't see either one of them. It was as if I was another person, a person that I knew all to well. Lisa slowly approached the door. I raised my right hand and did something that I been wanting to do for a minute…slap the shit out of her.

The slap made her spin around and then I hit her in the back of the head. It seemed as if everything was in slow motion. I knew that if this girl turned back around that I was gonna get beat up so I didn't stop hitting her. I jumped on her back and japed her out. I tried to choke her to death. Vint tried to get me off of her but adrenaline is a motherfucker. I started kneeing her in her back. I was determined to break this bitch down. She didn't know who she was fucking with. I wanted this chick to pee blood.

I saw Cheryl out of the corner of my eye. That's when I knew that I had calmed down. I was regaining focus. Cheryl cocked back that .25 Raven pointed it at Lisa and told her to get her big ass out of this

Cheryl Sutherland

house. Lisa stumbled to get up. She looked back at me and the word bitch slithered out of her mouth. Vint walked to the door and opened it for her. He slammed the door behind her.

Cheryl is the type of person who don't care what comes out her mouth, so she asked Vint what she needed to ask him.

"Why did that girl come here? Are you her *captain-save-a-ho* or what?"

"Naw, she only know where I stay at because she helped me and Tilak move this furniture in here." We all started to laugh 'cause she was kind of mannish. I was definitely out of breath but horny as hell. I looked at Vint and told him to go upstairs so we can do what we had planned to do before we were rudely interrupted.

We went upstairs and got into our king sized bed. I laid down as Vint began to rub my feet. It felt so good to get treatment like this. I let my mind drift as I thought about our lives together. I pictured us married with four or five kids together. Our house would be located out in the acreage somewhere. I tried to get into the mood but there were questions that I was dying to ask. So me being me I did.

"How do you know Lisa?" I asked. His eyes got big. He hesitated a moment and replied, "I know her from Tilak."

Chocolate Ty

"Well is it true about them messing around for a year."

"No…they been messing around for a couple of years on and off but for the last year he's been trying to wean himself off of you and on to her ugly ass." he joked.

"Can you tell me how everything went down and how it all boiled down to this?"

"Naw, I'm not going to do that Ty."

I said aggressively, "Why not that's the least you can do. You owe me that."

"Ty, on the real, you've been through too much and I don't want to hurt you more that you've already been hurt."

"What, you think that I can't handle it? I can. Trust me."

"That's what I'm afraid of Lil' Mike Tyson. But since you wanna know I'm going to tell you. It all started when you and Tilak first got together. You were still in school and all."

I wrapped my arms around him to hold on to him as he told me the secrets I never knew existed. I knew that I was going to get hurt by the truth but at least I'd know what happened and what the future held.

Vint continued, "I really liked you for Tilak. You were young but you had your head on straight.

──────────── **Cheryl Sutherland** ────────────

I knew he was fucking with Lisa then but he didn't want to be with her. See Lisa worked for Tilak at his automobile transportation company based out of an office in Juno. She been wanting him but she's like seven years older than Tilak, and Tilak wanted somebody young and fun.

"That's how I got into the picture. You know Flick and Flick know Terrance. Terrance always used to talk about Cheryl and her fly ass home girl which was you. Now, I told Tilak about what Terrance said and he was cool with scoping you."

He paused, his hands rubbing my arms as I held on to him.

"Now I know you used to see Tilak come up to your school and shit, that's because he was getting ready to put the moves on you. From jump Tilak was digging you. He was hard up on you from rip. He been jealous and possessive about you but he couldn't let you see that. That's why he convinced you to get your diploma at home because he was convinced that you had a boyfriend in school and before he take all that drama to the school he rather just take you out the school."

I interrupted, "Now it's beginning to make sense." His eyes looked at me. "Sorry. Please continue."

"Well that's when he had to tell Lisa that he

Chocolate Ty

wasn't feeling her and for her to stop calling him. He really wanted to be with you and only you. Now Lisa on the other hand was not going to take that shit lying down. She used to call me to call him and stupid shit like that. Now Lisa, a grown ass 31 year old woman and she round here keying his car and flattening his tires and all kinds of B.S. like that.

"I mean she tried calling and playing the role of she's gonna kill herself and all that but the day me and her fucked it was all over. Tilak was thru with her. He knew she set it all up, that's why he never got upset with me or at least he didn't show it at that time. Now the only reason why he got back with Lisa is that she came up on some money. She won a settlement hearing with Wal-Mart from a slip and fall accident. A $150,000 dollar slip and fall accident. Now I know that don't seem like a lot when it comes to Tilak but she was willing to blow it all on him. Now in his eyes he wanted the bread but he wanted you so he decided to have both. He never intended on you catching him with her. After her ends got low he was gonna leave her again. But when you caught him with her and broke it off with him, he lost it.

"He called me the same day that he hit you. He was crying and everything I mean I never heard him like that a day in my life. He just asked me to come over there because he was scared that you told the police everything that happened and he wanted me to be his alibi. I agreed just because he's my unk (uncle). I rode over there and he kept pacing back and forth. I didn't understand how a nigga could have all his emotions wrapped up in you when he was steady dealing with a whole 'nother broad.

"He told me that I had to help him. I was like, 'help you do what?' He was like it was nothing major, just to keep tabs on you. Since you didn't know what I looked like I was like "Cool, whatever" you know. I let him know the deal with you but I told him to just let it go. He didn't want to hear that shit. He knuckled up to me and all. This nigga was gone over you. Then he threw the fact that I fucked Lisa in my face and that I owe him one. So he took it a step further when he realized that you weren't playing and that you weren't coming back. He wanted me to date you then break up with you so you could be just as hurt as he was.

"But when he pulled that stunt at your apartment I knew that I couldn't let you go back to him. No woman deserved what he did to you and your friend. I figured whatever it takes, even if you're not with me, as long as you weren't with him. I knew that you needed someone to protect you and be there for you and I've never done that for any woman but I can do it for you. I still can't believe he did these things to you. I don't know how he thought that was gonna bring you back by torturing you but I guess he letting the wrong thing take over his mind."

"The night that I was supposed to leave and go to Virginia with Flick he sent me a text and told me to say goodbye to you that's why I was like fuck it I'm coming but it was too late. I know that bitch Lisa did that shit to your truck. That's why I invited her in so you could get a good look at her and how she was fucked up. You know what they say what goes around comes around and now it's time for Tilak to get his."

I saw Vint in a whole different light after he told me how it went down. It wasn't as serious as I was taking it. I felt as if we could get through this together. But in the back of my mind I knew that I couldn't trust him whole heartedly, it shouldn't have taken me to get shot and loose a baby for him to tell me this. I am going to chill but I got an eye open for him.

CHAPTER 18

When I woke up the next morning all I had on my mind was how to get Tilak out of my life. I knew that this would take a whole lot of deceiving and manipulation but it had to be done. Out of all the things Tilak put me through I just couldn't picture him dead. It wasn't in me to play God. I know that Vint had no problem with it but deep down inside I did.

I tried to think of other ways to get rid of him or for him to leave me alone. My mind was blank. I couldn't think of anything. I know that he probably thought I was dead but I know that ho Lisa done went and told him otherwise after last night. Well she'll get tired of him sooner or later. A bitch can only take so much.

I got up to brush my teeth and wash my face but the thoughts of Tilak just lingered in my head. It felt as if it would never stop. I went downstairs to make breakfast so I could focus on something else.

──────── **Cheryl Sutherland** ────────

Cheryl was still sleeping on the couch. I know the aroma of food would wake her up. I got the eggs, beef sausage, pancake mix and fruits together so I can start to prepare this feast. Just as soon as the pots and pans started clinking and clanking Cheryl sat up.

"What you about to make?"

"Some good old fashion breakfast." I said with a smile on my face.

"I know Vint didn't give you none last night so what you so happy about?"

"He told me. He actually told me the truth about the whole situation."

"Really? Did you have to beg or did he come right out with it?"

"Well, you know I had to ask but that was it. I asked and he told me. That's it. He must really be through with Tilak's ass."

"Hell I hope so. Get me a washcloth and a towel so I can freshen up."

"Girl you know where everything at."

Cheryl began to walk to the garage.

"Where you going?"

"Bitch, you know I stay with the over night bag in the trunk."

We both busted out laughing because she's been keeping an overnight bag with her ever since I met her.

We all got down on breakfast. It was something we haven't had in a while. All you could hear is the sound of lips smacking and forks scraping against the plates. As soon as we finished Vint lit up a joint. He dragged for a moment and exhaled a cloud of smoke. Of course Vint was the first person who had something to say.

"Baby, how bout Lisa called my phone this morning. She wanted to apologize for last night but I told her I didn't want to hear it and if she wanted you to know that she was sorry for that shit, she should call and tell you." he said as he passed the joint.

"And what did she say to that?" I said as I hit the joint.

"What could she say? She had no choice but to agree with me. That was her bad, not yours."

"Do you think she told Tilak that she saw me?"

"I really don't know but either way he gone."

I put my head down to that thought.

"Well I've been thinking about…you know, and I don't want you to do that anymore." I said hesitantly.

"Why not! All the shit he put you through. Why the hell not?" Cheryl said.

"Yeah baby, why not. What turned your spirit

─────────── **Cheryl Sutherland** ───────────

around?" Vint asked.

"Well number one, I can't have anyone's life on my hands...number two, I can't risk any one of you going to jail 'bout this nigga...and three, it's just unjust. He can do whatever he likes to me. It only makes me stronger. It makes all of us stronger."

"Make us stronger? Girl he gots to go. Shit maybe we can just get him locked up so we don't have to deal with his ass anymore," Cheryl suggested.

Everyone looked at each other as if that was the best suggestion made at that moment.

"Well, what y'all wanna do?" Cheryl asked.

"I wanna go with that plan. That way no one gets hurt, no one goes to jail except Tilak and no one has a guilty conscience. Tilak will be out of my life and I can watch the whole thing go down!"

Every one was down with that all we had to do now is come up with the master plan. A full-proof, error-proof plan. This was going to take some critical thinking because Tilak is on top of his shit. No one knew what he really did but everyone had ideas. We had to think of one reason that he would let someone into his mind, one weakness that he had.

What in the world was his Kryptonite?

It didn't take long to figure that out, it was

the power of the P-U-S-S-Y.

CHAPTER 19

For the next few days we sat and deliberated about how to get our plan into action. We knew that we could do it if we rationalized every situation. I knew that I had a couple of connections in law enforcement. I knew that Vint had a couple of street connections and I know that Cheryl had the bitch that could pull all this shit together. We all got on our jobs. We figured that this could take a couple of weeks so we were prepared for that wait. Vint made some phone calls so he could find out Tilak's whereabouts.

I had Cheryl to hit her homegirl up in VA and tell her the beat and she did. The next week we booked her a flight and she was on a plane in a heart beat. As long as everything was paid for including her, she was in the game room. Now that we have a decoy we need to let her and Tilak meet.

Vint had to call Lisa and find out what she told Tilak. She was being discreet at first but she finally told Vint everything. She was hiding from Tilak. She hadn't talked to him since he beat her down. She had a million and one questions to ask Vint and all he could do was assure her that he wouldn't let Tilak know where she was at.

As soon as Shavon touched down she was on top of her game. She stepped off the plane fly as hell. She had on a hard ass Parasuco outfit. Soon as she saw us we were right where we left off from the last time we saw each other. We filled her in on all the details and how everything was going down. We told her that the situation could be very dangerous but Shavon was a thrill seeker. Shavon didn't give a fuck. She was licensed to shoot a nigga. As long as she had her .22 she wasn't scared. I'm glad she wasn't because I had a little fear in my heart for her.

We figured that the only way that we could let Shavon and Tilak link up was if Lisa set him up in the right place at the right time. Lisa wasn't down with that but we finally convinced her to just call him and set up a date and we'll take care of the rest.

Lisa called him later on that night from a blocked number.

"Who da fuck is this!"

"Umm, it's me Lisa."

"Why you blocking your number. What you don't want me to get to you or something?"

"No, that's not it. I want to make up with you. I really miss you but if your going to be abusive towards me then forget it."

She knew she had him but to her surprise…

"Bitch! I don't want your ass. Who the fuck do you think you are, Tyrena! You think you a dime piece or something. Get the fuck off my phone!"

Click!

Lisa just stood there with her mouth agape. She couldn't believe she just got tried like that. She picked up the phone and called Vint.

"Hello."

"He doesn't want to see me any more." she said with tears in her eyes.

"Are you crying?"

"No. I'm just shocked."

Vint shook his head because he wasn't surprised at all. "Well at first if you don't succeed try again."

"No! I'm not going to put myself through that! The shame and humiliation…fuck him and fuck you too!"

Click

Lisa hung up the phone abruptly. Vint was worried that their plan wasn't going to go through.

Cheryl Sutherland

He really didn't care because he would just go with the first plan. Vint called me to tell me the news.

"Baby, how bout Lisa just called me and said Tilak told her that he don't want to see her."

"WHAT! What do you mean he doesn't want to see her?"

"Just like I said baby but its okay we'll just go with option one."

"No! I want that nigga to suffer and taking his life is too good for him, that's the easy way out. He needs to go through the same hell I've been going through. I know his pretty ass won't last one day in prison. What the fuck can we do now?"

"Man, then we'll just torture him before we take his ass out."

"No! Don't you get it? A couple of hours of that can't compare to me losing a good friend, him stalking me, shooting me and making me loose my child. Not once, but twice. All that shit was on his hands and I know he don't feel no way about it but I do and death is just too good for him. Baby you got to feel me."

"I do. But..." Vint couldn't even say anything he knew deep down inside he knew she was right. He just wanted it over A.S.A.P. "Okay baby if you come up with something hit me up. I'll be at the house."

─────────────── **Chocolate Ty** ───────────────

"Well I'm on my way home anyways. I'll see you when I get there."

Cheryl could tell by the look on my face that something got screwed up. Cheryl sat up in the truck and asked me what was wrong. I explained the situation and that they had to think of another way to get Tilak and Shavon to meet. Cheryl looked at me with empathy in her eyes because she knew what I was thinking but didn't come right out and say it.

We pulled up to Vint's crib in silence. We walked through the door and Vint was sitting at the bar rolling up a phattie. As soon as Cheryl saw Vint she busted out and told him what I had been thinking but never said.

"Vint, I think your girl is going to make contact with Tilak."

Vint stood up and walked over to me and held me in his arms.

"No, you're not going to do that Ty. You're not going to do it."

"Why not? You know he'll stop at nothing to put me out of my "misery" and as you know misery loves company," I tried to joke.

"Man, you know he thinks that you're dead and as long as he thinks that you're safe."

"I'm not safe, Vint. We live in the same fucking

city. One day we will bump heads. And I will be scared everyday until I do something about it. I don't want to spend the rest of my life looking over my shoulder and peeping around corners. I can't live like that. If your truck didn't have these tints on it I would probably confine myself to this house, and I refuse to do that again."

Vint just stepped back and looked at his girl. He kissed her on the forehead. He knew that she was a soldier and after all it was just one phone call. They didn't have to meet. Tilak didn't have to know where they were. It could be a safe move and if it made Ty feel better about her self then why not. Vint handed her the phone and Cheryl snatched it out of his hand.

"What did you do that for?" Vint exclaimed.
"I'm not going to sit here and watch my friend commit suicide. That's what I'm doing."
"I'm not going to commit anything! Cheryl just give me the phone. It's just one phone call. I'll block the number."
"I just want you to think about it. Right now you're in shock and your adrenaline is rushing and you're making rash decisions. Just sleep on it, please."

Chocolate Ty

    I thought about it and agreed. Besides, he would know that something was up if me and Lisa called within hours of each other. We all agreed that the phone call would be made the following day and I would set everything up for me and Tilak to meet.

CHAPTER 20

That night I kept having nightmares. I couldn't sleep at all. The memories of Tilak trying to kill me haunted me in my sleep. It just replayed over and over again in my head. I was sweating and my clothes were soaking wet. I got up to change and as I got back in the bed I saw that Vint was awake.

He turned to me and said "If you don't want to do this then don't. I'm telling you we can find anyone to do this. I just don't want to lose you and I definitely don't want anymore drama in your life. I love you."

My heart dropped as the words poured out his mouth. But the fact of the matter was that I did want to do it. In my heart I knew that I could reel that bastard in, hook, line and sinker. But was it worth it? Damn right it was.

I looked at Vint. I could see all the love in his eyes. I knew he meant every word. Just because I knew that, I knew that he wouldn't let Tilak harm me.

    I rolled on top of him. We haven't had sex in three weeks and I felt as if my body needed this. I just laid on top of him for a minute or two. I still hadn't answered his question but he knew how I felt and that I was going to go through with it. I kissed him on the neck. He looked at me and he knew it was on. He held my head steady and gave me the most passionate kiss I had ever experienced in my life. My heartbeat started to rise. The tingling began in my sacred spot. His hands began to caress my back. He squeezed and massaged my ass until he could here the sound of my pussy getting wet as my cheeks parted.

    The way he kissed me made me feel the love that he just shortly expressed. He rolled over so that I was now on the bed. He kissed and undressed me from head to toe. Not skipping one body part or limb. He got down to my feet and rubbed them and kissed them. I was in ecstasy already.

    I was feening for the dick but he made me wait.

    He slid his tongue up my thigh as it made its way to my womanly abyss. Soon as I felt the warmth of his breath I let out a quiet moan. I knew that he could hear me but I didn't care. He licked my clit as if it was a tasty treat that he deserved for being a

Chocolate Ty

good boy. He knew how to work that tongue just for my satisfaction. I was about to cum as he stopped. He knew he was teasing me and that made me want him even more.

He sat up and took his boxers off. He grabbed my hand and placed it on his manhood. I knew what to do, so I sat up behind him and began to jack his dick. He always liked the touch of my soft hand on him. I glided my hand very slowly up and down his shaft. He reached back so he could feel me. I maneuvered my way to the front of him and pushed him so he could lay back. I put my knees on the floor so that I could be leveled. I licked his thighs as he began to tremble. I reached his balls and began to lick them. I like to do this to him because it makes him go crazy. He grabbed onto the sheets as my tongue hit his spot and then I wet my tongue and glided it up his shaft to the tip of his head.

My mouth was warm and I knew he'd think it was the best feeling in the world. His erection was a new record. It barely fit into my mouth. I did what I do best and plunged back and forth on it. He was a wreck. He tried to call out to me but I would just hum and he would stop. It was getting to the point that I had to get on. He made me feel like I was the only woman who ever made him feel this way.

His juices started to seep into my mouth. It

had its own unique taste, not bitter but not sweet either, it was just right for me.

I slowly let my mouth rise off him. He grabbed my hair as if to say take it very slow. When I got up he held me by the waist. He lifted one leg up and placed it on the bed. He took the other one and did the same. He slowly placed me on his penis and maneuvered me up and down. He felt so good inside me. I just wanted to stay this way for the rest of the night. He continued to move me until he felt as if he was going to cum. He held it back and placed me back on the bed. He kissed me in the mouth again. He stared in my eyes and, softly said, "I love you."

A tear ran down the side of my face and I could barely get the words out. I told him that I loved him too.

He began to penetrate me slowly. I could tell he was enjoying it as much as I was. Every time he would draw back I felt so empty and when he would come back in I felt whole again. The way he moved, so passionately, I could tell we were making love. He continued to slow-stroke me until I couldn't take it anymore. He kept staring at me as if he couldn't believe that it was me he was making love to. I grabbed him around the waist and hiked my legs up so he could get in good. He could feel the change. He began to speed up his pace just a little bit. He always amazed me on how he could keep his rhythm going. I felt my walls beginning to throb. This would be it, the orgasm of my lifetime. He kept stroking and he gave me a kiss on the lips. All I could do was call out his name and at that point I hit my mark. My legs were shaking; my toes were curled so tightly I thought they were going to break off.

He lifted me up off the bed and in the air. He bounced me up and down on his one eyed monster. I was out of my mind. He would grind and move while he bounced me up and down, making sure to get every corner. Then I could feel his penis swell up as he let go inside of me. It was so warm and moist. He gently laid me on the bed with his penis still inside me. I could feel his body jerking and penis pulsating. He lay on top of me breathing hard. He kissed my lips and then my forehead and then he slowly pulled out of me.

He laid there beside me and held my hand. He whispered in my ear that he loves me and he will be there to protect me in whatever decision I choose. That made me feel safe and secure and with him in my corner I am willing to take this obstacle out of my life for good.

CHAPTER 21

Well, the day is here.

It was 11 o' clock in the morning. I knew that Tilak was out and about. I didn't think that I would be so nervous. But I was. Vint and I sat in the living room and I picked up the house phone. I knew that Cheryl would be hot if I made this phone call without her being there to hold my hand but I couldn't wait. The anticipation was killing me.

I picked up the phone and pressed *67 and dialed his seven digits. It rang and rang. I hung up the phone. Vint asked me what happened. I lied and told him that I got the voicemail. He knew that I was lying but he played along. He told me to wait an hour or so then give him a call back. I agreed to that 'cause by that time Cheryl would have came by and I would definitely have the courage to do it.

We went to go get some breakfast at Friendly's. We were so comfortable in thought that the bullshit was almost over that we let a couple of hours pass before we even realized it. We got up and paid the tab.

We walked out to the truck and as we started to pull off, Tilak ass was pulling up. He waved Vint down. Vint told me to lay my seat back. I did.

"Wassup, Jit? Long time no hear from. How's life?" Tilak said with an evil grin on his face.

"What do you want?"

"You heard from ya girl lately?" he requested.

"Naw, why?"

"Well I heard through the grape vine that she wants to see me." he said as Lisa sat up in the seat on the passenger side.

Vint looked at her and kept the poker face going "Well I haven't talked to her. Tell your resources to find her and holla at her."

"You sure Jit or are you lying to ya uncle? You wouldn't lie for that bitch would you?"

"Does it even matter what I say. If you think that I'm lying when you ask me a question then don't ask." Vint snapped back.

"Boy! Who you getting slick with! Don't you know that I'll break yo little ass nigga!"

Vint just looked at him and rode off. He followed us for a block or two then turned off and went his own way. I just looked at him with fear in my eyes. Vint knew that the sound of his voice sent trembles in my heart. How the hell could I carry on a conversation with him?

"Don't get discouraged baby we are going to get through this."

Just those words gave me the courage to get through the 5 seconds that I would have to talk to him on the phone. I told Vint to go to Cheryl's house so we can call him. A few minutes later we pulled up to the fire department and police vehicles blocking Cheryl's roadway. My heart dropped. I jumped out the car and began to run towards the house just to see Cheryl sitting outside watching her next door neighbor's house go up in flames.

"Oh my God!" I said falling to my knees.

"Girl I know. I couldn't believe it either. So close to home." she said in disbelief.

"Let's go to the truck we have a dilemma." I instructed.

She followed me to the truck. Vint was walking in our direction. He ran to Cheryl and gave her a hug. She pushed him off of her while telling him that it was the house next door. We all gathered in the truck and told her what just went down in the parking lot of Friendly's, a secluded restaurant that served down south home cooking. She couldn't believe that the bitch he just said that he didn't want to fuck with anymore done snitched on us.

―――――――――――― Cheryl Sutherland ――――――――――――

"Now how were we going to get this asshole?" Cheryl questioned.

"Oh we still gonna go through with our plan. We're just going to have to wait for a while. What I need to do is let him see me then make that phone call." I plotted.

"You're taking it too far now!" Vint said.

"I agree." Cheryl contributed.

"Well right now I don't care. Shit, my birthday coming up, I can't be scared thinking that I have to watch my back all night long in order to have a good time. I want this issue taken care of now. I'm not trying to do anything drastic; I'm just talking about a pass by in the mall or in the grocery store. Cheryl, I will appreciate it if you come with me. Then I'll set up the date and put Shavon on."

"Boo yah! We got his ass." Cheryl said excitedly.

Everyone agreed. The next day Cheryl and I went everywhere, bouncing from mall to mall. We didn't want Vint to call because if we show up where he was after Vint's phone call then he would know that some thing was up. So we just had a girl's day out and if we were confronted with Tilak we would feel safe because we were in a public setting.

Day one was a flop. No sign of Tilak any where. But we didn't loose hope. Day two would be a better day. The next day Cheryl felt a little under the weather which meant that Terrance came back into her life. She was always 'sick' when it came time for us to do something and he didn't want her to go. I never minded it and got ready anyway.

"Where's Cheryl?" Vint asked as I dried my body.

"She home waiting on me."

Vint gave me the eye "You sure?"

"Uh huh." I just talked to her."

"Well let me call her just to double check."

He got up and grabbed his phone. I wanted to stop him but if I did then he would assume that I'm lying and I was but he didn't need to find that out. He looked at me as the phone rang. I just stared back at him. He closed his phone, stood up and walked over towards me. I took a step back.

He looked at me in a way that he knew that I was going to do something wrong. He opened those beautiful lips and said, "Ty, I hope you not lying to me. And I hope you know what you doing. I don't want anything to happen to you. Can you understand that? "

I put my head down 'cause I knew that I was wrong. Anything could happen to me out there but I was being so hard headed. I knew that. I really wanted to get this over with and I was willing to sacrifice my self for that. I had to get it together. I opened my mouth to tell Vint what was really good.

At that time his phone rang. He kept his eye on me as he picked it up.

"What up Vint." Cheryl said.

"Oh, nothing much Cheryl, was happening?"

"Nothing, I'm on my way over there. Is Ty ready?"

"Yeah, she's getting ready now. I thought she was coming to pick you up?"

"She was 'cause I thought Terrance was gonna take the car but he changed his mind."

"You still fucking with that clown. Girl you gonna get enough. I guess I'll see you when you get here."

"Aight."

My eyes lit up. My girl always had my back.

"Why you looking like you just won some lottery or something?" Vint asked.

I conjured up, "Nothing, I just didn't want to make that trip in your truck."

"Yeah I bet. She just lying for you but I can't prove it. Man y'all been friends for too long. It's like y'all have E.S.P. or something." he said as he turned and walked off.

I ran and jumped on his back. We both laughed and got caught up in the moment. I loved him so much and I was finally assured that he felt the same way about me.

CHAPTER 22

Cheryl and I set off to find our mark. We first went to the malls in the Palm Beaches. We then went to the outskirts of town with no luck. We were like animals trying to find our prey. I was actually hoping to run into him so I can get my part over with. We drove around for 10 hours trying to find this bastard.

I noticed a car following us for most of our trip. I made several phone calls to Vint to let him now our progress in this manhunt and about the suspect car. He told me to never mind it and gave me the inspiration to keep going.

We went to the Boynton Beach Mall and anticipated to see him. I had to strut my stuff as I walked through that mall just in case we did see him. I knew I was doing it and would come face to face with this asshole but all I got was a couple of numbers from some teenagers. We sat at the food court as a look of frustration came over my face. I

Cheryl Sutherland

really wanted to give up. I wanted to let him win. I guess the anticipation of me getting my revenge was taking a toll on me. I signaled to Cheryl that I was ready to go home.

On our way to the house I received a call from Vint. He sounded very ecstatic. I tried to calm him down put he just rushed through the conversation. I told Cheryl to speed it up so we can hurry up and get to the house to find out what all the commotion was about.

We pulled into the driveway. I jumped out of Cheryl's Benz and we hurried to the house. The look on Vint's face made all of us smile. He told us to hurry up and sit down and we did so.

"How bad do you want all of this to be over Ty?" Vint asked.

I sat there with a look of "could you believe this nigga" on my face.

"Very badly dear." I responded.

"Well, ya boy Tilak just called me. He wants me to do a run for him. Now I have to go up north like I planned to do before. Now if I make this run for him he said that he would leave us alone."

I sat with a puzzled look on my face and blurted out.

"He could've done that shit from jump. Why the hell did he make me go through all this for a filthy fucking run? What did he all of a sudden loose interest in my life or what? I can't believe this asshole. What did you tell him Vint?"

"I told him Yeah."

"You told him yeah. What if this shit is a setup?"

"It can't be, he didn't even insist on you going Ty."

"Yeah but what if you leave and he try that stunt again, then what."

"You got Cheryl, and Terrance don't forget about ya girl Shavon either."

"What they gonna do when he creep up on my ass Vint!"

"Baby he not gonna do that. Trust me," he said.

"What is he paying you to leave me?" I said with tear-filled eyes.

"No, no Ty he guaranteed me this. He put it on his life. Bay he's tired. He know that I'm gonna be here for you and I ain't going no where. It's too late. I'm here for you and I love you. He knows that now."

"When is it going down?"

"We leaving at eleven." He said hesitantly.

"TONIGHT! But my birthday is in three more days, how you going to leave like that?"

Cheryl Sutherland

"I know bay, I should be back by then. Okay how 'bout this, either way I'm going to make it up to you."

"Whatever. Hold up, wait one minute who is we?"

"Me and Flick. Why, is that a problem? You know he can drive those distances and he can get there in 12 hours flat." Vint protested.

I just had to walk up to him and give him a hug and hope that he was right. I was once again putting my life in his hands. He kissed me on the forehead and ran upstairs.

Cheryl agreed to stay with me while Vint made his trip. I felt a little more protected but not fully. We both invited Shavon over and told her not to forget her baby. I couldn't believe all this was happening in a matter of hours. I went upstairs to help Vint pack while we went over all the rules and regulations of this trip.

"You know if anything seem fishy or you don't feel right about something don't do it." I let him know.

"I didn't feel right bout what Tilak wanted me to do to you, I mean him paying me to be with you but I did it anyways and I'm not regretting it at all."

"That's different you followed your heart for love."

Chocolate Ty

"It's no different. I'm doing the same thing right now. I'm doing this because I love you. I want all this to be over with."

I reached across the bed and grabbed his hand. I pulled him close to me. I gave him a kiss to let him now that everything was going to be alright. He grasped my waist and yanked me over towards him. He kissed me and made me lie on the bed. I knew what he wanted and as his woman I was obliged to give it to him.

He hiked my skirt up and pulled my panties to the side. All I could do was think about kinky sex. He gave my twat a kiss and made it real moist for me, the way that he knows how to do it. He entered into his house and let me know that daddy's home. He fucked me so good that I started to wonder how long it will last. I always enjoyed the end when he left his pipe inside of me and let his plumbing drain into my canal.

I always figured that if your man left home happy that he wouldn't have to look for love in the streets. I always tried to live by that.

CHAPTER 23

It's been three hours since my baby left me. I stayed calling his cell phone. In my heart, I really felt as if it was a set up that Tilak was trying to pull. I prayed that God protected him and Flick on his way there and back.

In the mean time Cheryl, Shavon and I were deliberating on how to go about this new life for me. These girls are optimistic and if I ever needed some positive advice it would definitely come from them. They suggested that I move. I promised that I would stay close enough for visits but far enough to miss Riviera. We laughed and smoked. Vint left us a QP of Chocolate Tah so we took advantage of that situation. We all came to an agreement of going to get our hair, nails and toes done tomorrow. We figured that we've been rocking ponytails and hair buns long enough and we need to step our game up. I made a call to Ms. Keisha, the secretary, at Universal Image for our appointments. I knew that

―――――――――― **Cheryl Sutherland** ――――――――――

it was a last minute thing but she decided to squeeze us in.

The next morning we woke up at 6 a.m. so we could be at the shop by 7 a.m. I'm just glad that we have three bathrooms. Women do take a while to get dressed. I figured that the only thing that needs to look good on me was my outfit and I know that my stylist Chisha would take care of the rest. We finally piled up into Vint's Chevy Avalanche at 6:45 and took off to Universal Image Hair Salon.

We pulled up right on time, Ms. Keisha was just opening up shop. If you arrived two minutes late your appointment was gone. We had an appointment with Chisha and she already had someone in the chair and four more waiting. But we knew that we weren't going to make one move because she was the best and was absolutely worth the wait.

Chisha put the girl that she was doing under the dryer and called me up. I happily skipped to her booth as we engaged in small talk. I told her that my birthday was coming up and that she had to tighten me up. She looked at me as if I was insulting her but I didn't care I was going to be here by myself for my birthday. She felt where I was coming from though.

Chisha combed the relaxer through my hair

and complained on how long it took for me to come back and see her and how nappy my roots were. I knew it but still, I didn't care, that's the only reason she decided to do me first is that my hair is the thickest and will take the longest to do. She always had a rhythm. She did everything in rotation, while I'm deep conditioning, she would hit up my two stick girls.

Time just seemed to fly by. By time Chisha wrapped my hair to sit under the dryer; it was already 11 o' clock. While under the dryer I decided to call my baby. I went into my Gucci purse and picked up my cell phone and I had four missed calls accompanied by three voice mails and one text message; all from Vint of course. I checked my text message first. It read:

Babe, we made it down. Holla back ☺

I then checked my voice mails. It was just him telling me to call him back at my earliest convenience. I anticipated hearing his voice but he didn't answer my call. I left him a message and told him that I was at the hair salon and for him to call me back as soon as possible. I ended the call with joy in my heart. Just the thought of him making it up there safe was relieving.

I had to sit under the dryer for two hours. I eventually fell asleep under the hood, a big no-no in the hood. But luckily my girls were with me. When Chisha came and woke me up to let her finish my hair I was in another world.

The shop was packed now. All the bootleggers and gossipers where in the shop holding it down and telling everyone's business. I got a couple of stares and whispers but I held my head up and strutted to her chair. She did the final touches and had a sister looking tight. I told her to arch my eyebrows and wax my slightly grown-in mustache, after that I would be the meaning of perfection. It was now 1:13 p.m. a time that I will never forget. I went into my purse and saw that my phone had 21 missed calls in the midst of two hours. It was all Vint. I hurried and called him back. He picked up the phone on the first ring.

"Baby I need you big time."

"What happened?"

"I got a connect and I need you to fly up here get this package and drive back down. Tilak is going to leave one of his cars in the garage at City Place. When you get here I'll tell you the rest but it need to be all done by 3 o' clock tomorrow afternoon."

"So I need to leave like now?"

Chocolate Ty

"Right now! Look, this is it. I won't have to deal wit nobody else. We on top baby, we on top, we won't need a middle man cutting into my bricks. It comes straight to me, I'm going to be that nigga ya' heard. While you here we can do a little celebrating you know what I mean?"

"I hope you talking about my birthday."

"Yep. I'll have my B show us around VA so we can get our party on."

"Okay, I'm there."

I was so anxious to hurry and get my hair done. Cheryl and Shavon could tell that I was the bearer of good news. They kept signaling me to tell them what was up. I told them that they would find out later. I always knew that you could never speak about business in a public place like a hair salon. Your business will be on the freeway before you jump on. We all got our wigs flipped and we were out the door. Of course Chisha was happy because we just paid her enough money to pay her rent.

We all piled up in the Avalanche and went to Crazy Buffet; a Chinese restaurant that had mad food. I discussed what they needed to know at that time. The only reason why I discussed it in that restaurant is that they have a sound-proof conference room.

Most people don't know that but I learned a

few tricks from Tilak.

CHAPTER 24

On this day I was excited because my homegirls were excited. I told the girls what was up and they were down. Just like that. I knew I had a squad and they were gonna be my back bone through all this. Only death can do us part. I reserved three tickets on Southwest Airlines, each one departing at 4:55 pm that evening. I hurried and packed my Louis Vuitton suitcase and duffle bag. Cheryl and Shavon were already packed from the night before. We hauled ass to the Palm Beach International Airport and barely made our flight.

On the plane we discussed what we had to discuss and Shavon decided to stay when we arrived because we had everything handled and no longer needed her assistance. We touched down in Norfolk at 6:40 pm. We went straight to Enterprise car rentals and purchased a Dodge Durango. We dropped Shavon off at her crib and called Vint. He

Cheryl Sutherland

said he was in Ingleside so we jetted over there.

Cheryl still remembered how to get around Norfolk. We pulled up to the Citgo gas station on Ingleside and Virginia Beach Boulevard and Vint came out of a Lexus with a suitcase. He jumped in the back seat of our ride while Flick and their new found kingpin followed us in his 2005 Lexus LS430. Shit, that model wasn't even out on the streets yet.

Vint instructed me to go to the Waterside Marriot on East Main Street and I did as I was instructed. I could feel the adrenaline pulsating throughout my body. It was actually fun going on a run. I don't know why I've always been so afraid to go. We arrived at our destination. The hotel was banging. We walked around a little bit and went to our designated room. There was food and drinks already there not to mention the Ziploc bag full of weed.

My eyes grew big as I examined each and everything going on at that particular time. Soon as I spotted the weed I walked over and opened the bag. The smell was incredible. The weed looked kind of fuzzy and had a tint to it. So I asked what it was. The kingpin said lobo or lobster is another name for it. Cheryl and I hurried and rolled a couple of joints while the fellas had their meeting in the other room.

Chocolate Ty

We blazed up not even thinking about them. We fogged up the room within in minutes. The weed was so good. It made you high without feeling sleepy or unearthed. You just got blazed. By the time they came out they were wondering what happened to the joints. Me and Cheryl looked at each other and began laughing. We rolled up three more joints for them. They sat and got blazed while Cheryl and I got even higher from contact smoke.

Cheryl and I got a little nap in before we decided to get dressed. It was the day before my birthday and I figured when the clock strikes midnight I need to be on somebody's dance floor shaking my ass like a stripper. I tried to wake Vint up but he was knocked out. I knew one thing that would wake him up though. Some slow head by the nightstand. Luckily he was already in his boxers and sleeping on his back. I maneuvered his penis out of the slit in the boxer shorts and began to rub his dick. It's hard to get the response that you want when the dick's on soft but it does have a mind of its own. I kept stroking him nice and slow making sure to tighten my grip just a little bit when I got towards the tip. He began to get erect and I seized the opportunity to make love to him with my mouth.

He moved around a little bit and I knew that I had him. I let my teeth graze his manhood while pulling up and made my tongue precede my lips on the way back down. He woke up and looked at me with a big kool-aid grin on his face. All I saw was the gold teeth through my peripheral. I just pretended that he was still sleep. I sucked and slurped on him until I felt his penis increasing in size in my mouth.

He pulled my face from off of him and told me to get on. I obliged, my pussy was soaking wet anyways. I slid onto his cock and began to ride him like no tomorrow. I was on point and on beat. I rode him and did my famous *turn-around-while-still-on-the-dick* move. He loved it when I would just bounced that ass on him while he smacked and rubbed my ass or put his finger in my butt, something that was cool by me. I knew that we were loud because I heard the others starting to rustle around in the living room in the suite. When we finished our little escapade we got into the shower and took our time and bathed each other.

I came out in a pink and beige dress from BCBG. It was almost summer so the weather was right for me to put this dress on. I walked into the living room to put my shoes on and everyone started laughing. I guess they were still high 'cause they already knew that Vint and I loved to make love no matter where we were.

Chocolate Ty

The kingpin took us to a nightspot call Shadows. He said that all kind of celeb's be in there like Allen Iverson, Timberland, Missy and the list went on. So know I was super hyped on getting into the club. The kingpin figured that he was going to show us where the club was then leave to go change and link back up with us. By time we got to the club the line was wrapped way around the building. I felt disgusted. I really wanted to go. I pushed out my bottom lip and let out a sigh.

"What's that for Ty? We're going in okay!" Vint said.

"I am not going to wait in that line!"

Just as I spoke those words the kingpin came to my door and told us to get out so he can let us into the club. I started dancing in my seat and jumped out of the Dodge Durango truck. We followed the kingpin past the extended line and to the security guard who looked as if he didn't even work there.

"What up, fam?" the security guard said while jumping to his feet and giving the kingpin a pound.

"Shit. What you not working tonight or you on your break?" the kingpin stated.

"It ain't like that. What up? They wit you?"

"Yeah, make sure they get whatever they want from the bar it's on me."

Cheryl Sutherland

"Bet."

We all walked past the security guard as he gave Vint and Flick pounds and gave Cheryl and me handshakes. I walked into the club and the first person that I saw was the nigga I wanted to have my first child from...A.I. he was so fine. His diamonds were sparkling in the club as he sat there and sipped on a beverage with his security guards right by his side. If I wasn't there with Vint I would be trying to get at homeboy.

I had a ball at the club. They had male strippers and all. The music was on point as well as the drinks. I danced for a long time on the dance floor until I saw a chick in Vint's face trying to dance with him. He kept trying to move away from her but she was on him. I politely walked over there and pulled him away from her. He threw his hands around my neck and stared to dance with me. We grinded on each other and kissed and hugged until the music stopped and the deejay spoke into the mic.

"If we have nay birthday people in the house I need you to make some noise!"

A roar of screams and shrieks filled the club including my own. I turned to Vint to see him smiling at me.

The deejay continued...

Chocolate Ty

"Well the clock is about to strike 12 so on the count of three I want you to sing Happy Birthday with me in dedication to all the people who made it to see another year."

My eyes instantly filled with tears when the deejay said that.

I was lucky, very lucky, to live to see another birthday. I guess Vint sensed my sadness because he began to hug me while my back was turned to him. He gave me a kiss on the cheek while the club counted down. Cheryl had found Shavon in the club and ran over to count to me.

"One, two, three...Happy birthday to you, happy birthday to you..."

I nestled in Vint's arms while he sung the song in my ear. Cheryl and Shavon sang and winked at me.

Vint reached into his pocket and pulled out a ring. He grabbed my left hand and placed the ring on my finger. I tried to hold the tears back but they came out anyways. I turned and gave him the biggest hug that I could muster up. He mouthed the words "Will you?" and nodded towards the ring and I nodded yes.

"Happy birthday, happy birthday to you...I...I...I...say, say, say. Now what's that birthday month again..." the deejay had thrown in

Cheryl Sutherland

Uncle Luke's infamous birthday jam song.

The club went wild as all clubs do when one of Luke's or a Two Live Crew record is thrown on the turntables. Cheryl and Shavon ran to the dance floor and took it over. I shook and popped on Vint until I felt his dick get hard. I was in another world, I didn't care how ghetto it was that he proposed to me at a nightclub in a city that we will probably never see again; it was that it was just me and him in our own world. I didn't have to watch my back from Tilak, or the ugly twins-Trina and Carmen or Lisa or anybody else that hated on me. I was at ease and I was drunk, the perfect combination.

The next day I was hung over. I didn't even have official birthday sex. I just sat around in the hotel room showing off my ring to Cheryl. She kept waving me off but I knew that she was happy for me. Vint and the kingpin went and took care f some "paperwork" and "litigations" while Cheryl and I went out to eat and shopped around for a little bit. We just wanted to waste time before we hit the highway.

We figured that if we get on I-95 at midnight then we could be back in Palm Beach around 1 o'clock the next afternoon. By time we finished shopping and site seeing we only had three and a half hours to get some rest. That was easy for Cheryl to do. She can fall asleep in two seconds flat. When Vint came back he had the kingpin and Flick with him looking very pleased. I figured everything went according to plan. I told him lets go to bed so he and I went to sleep on the pullout couch while Cheryl and Flick slept in the bedroom. The kingpin slept on the chaise.

It felt as if I just fell asleep in the arms of my man before the alarm on my phone went off. I got up and walked to the bathroom to wash my face and take a shower. I felt as if I was still high. That was some good ass weed.

When I got out of the shower I woke Cheryl up to do the same. I could tell she was still high by her sluggish actions.

When we finally pulled ourselves together it was almost one in the morning. I woke Vint up so he could walk us to the car. He let me know that he would be home in two days tops. I gave him a kiss and he gave me all the information that I had to know in order to make this transaction a successful one. He pleaded for me to be careful. Cheryl shouted out that I would and demanded me to get this show on the road. We took off in the midnight air. At first it was easy because we were excited to get home and have all the bullshit over. I felt exceptionally well because I was able to help my man in his time of need with no questions asked.

CHAPTER 25

Cheryl instructed me to do the speed limit while traveling through Emporia, a city in Virginia that's known for having the sheriff and police officers out ALL THE TIME and they would pull you over for doing four miles over the speed limit. I am glad that I did listen because 'troll was deep and posted up everywhere. We made it onto I-95 safely and we headed south. I knew that we were home free. We stopped for gas in Raleigh, North Carolina.

This damn truck was a gas guzzler, soon as I got to an exit where they sold gas Cheryl and I switched seats and I told her that we would switch again when we arrived in Florida or had to fill up again. Cheryl started off doing a hundred for about an hour straight. Then she started to get sleepy. The next thing I knew she was doing like 45 miles per hour on I-95. I politely told her to pull over at the next rest stop and I would drive until we needed another fill then she was gonna drive. So she said

Cheryl Sutherland

that she would get a cat nap in now and be well rested for her turn.

I pulled out of the rest area and jumped back on I-95.

We were in South Carolina and basically in the home stretch only seven hours to go, at the most. I set the truck on cruise control and let it ride at 85 mph. I switched to another radio station. After 40 minutes I saw the beautiful sign that said "Welcome to Georgia" I knew we were home. I woke Cheryl up and told her that gas was low so get her stretches in and get ready to drive. Of course she said okay.

I tried to read the signs that instructed me to the nearest gas station and that's when it all went down. I looked in my rear view mirror and saw the blue lights going off. I damn near shitted in my pants. I looked around and saw that I still had the cruise control on. I started to mash out and just keep going but that was unnecessary. I figured that he was going to give me a ticket and I would be on my way. Plus I'm a female, who would expect me to be trafficking?

But this cracker was an asshole. He made me and Cheryl get out of the car. He called for back up and patted us down from head to toe. Cheryl was crying I couldn't cry because I just knew that Tilak had something to do with this. But how? He

Chocolate Ty

still thought that Vint was making this run for him. He didn't even know that I rented a car. I finally saw the reason why I don't go on runs.

After the police did what they had to do, they told us to get back in the vehicle. We did. That was it, a ticket and an experience.

Trick me.

The officer knocked on the door and asked me if he could search the car. The look I gave him read guilty. Cheryl sat back and asked why. His smart ass gonna get slick and say "because I feel like it".

Cheryl snapped back and said that he needed a warrant for that. He stepped back and laughed and made us get back out the truck. I pinched Cheryl on the arm and told her that I was gonna haul ass if he find out what's in the suitcase. She was down with it.

The officer went through the suitcases and after what felt like an eternity yelled out, "BINGO"!

...and that was our cue.

We both flexed in opposite directions. I forgot that Cheryl's Jamaican ass was on the track team. She was out of sight before I could get a good start. I heard all the officers screaming for me to stop. I heard gun shots but knew that they were warning shots. I ran with all my might but that wasn't good enough. All it took was for one officer to tackle my ass and all of them piled up on me. They warned me to stop resisting or they would have to use mace. Breathing heavily they read me my rights and told me what I was being arrested for.

Thank God I wasn't in Palm Beach 'cause they would've tasered the hell out of my ass with their old trusty TASER® guns.

CHAPTER 26

The holding cell was colder than a motherfucker.

I already felt violated from the in depth search that the stumpy, old, corrections officer gave me. Her hair was knotty and her breath was humming and I think that she knew it 'cause every five seconds she was in my face, saying shit that I didn't want to hear. I was tired and frustrated. I couldn't wait until it was my turn to use the phone. It still felt as if I was in a dream but the reality of this matter would hit me soon.

I called Vint and he was shocked. He said that he was on his way down there but it would be a couple of hours. I jokingly told him okay and that I would be there when he gets here.

It felt like an eternity before they called out my name. They took my pictures, made me shower in their nasty ass, grimy stalls that had all types of mildew and mold in it. Then they assigned me to a

Cheryl Sutherland

cell with hard ass bunk beds and a stainless steel toilet and sink. The positive part about the whole situation was that I had a blanket now.

The icing on the cake was when they told me that I had no bond until court tomorrow. All I heard were the words "no bond" echo throughout the courthouse. Those words kept repeating in my head and the room started spinning around me.

The next morning they woke all the inmates up at five o' clock in the morning for court that started at 9 am. I ate some sorry ass raisin bran cereal and an apple. My hair was a mess but when we reached the courthouse I felt at ease. I waited for the bailiff to call my docket number. When he did, the first thing I did when I got into the courtroom was look around for Vint. There he was in an all white linen suit looking so good that I creamed my panties. To take my focus off him I looked next to him and he was with some white guy that I assumed was his lawyer.

The judge asked the DA what my charges were and when they began to read them off. They made it seem worse that what it really was. Resisting arrest, possession of cocaine, drug trafficking, wreck less driving, intent to distribute and/or sell, assault on an officer and not wearing a seat belt. Vint eyes were full of tears, he had to put his head down in his hand so I couldn't tell but we were bonded and I felt his pain. This was my life though, and he couldn't feel worse than I did.

All the promises he made to keep me safe seemed as if they were washed down the drain. The judge set my bail at $200,000.00 I felt my heart drop all the way down to my pinky toe. Later on that day I spoke with the lawyer. I lied and told him that I didn't know that drugs were in that suitcase. I told him that that suitcase wasn't even a part of my luggage set. I had a Louis Vuitton set and that was a Samsonite suitcase. We talked for a while and he didn't mention Cheryl's name…If he didn't say anything about Cheryl neither was I.

He said that he could get me out that day. He also informed me that I have had undercover Federal agents following me for the past month or so trying to get me connected with Tilak. I couldn't believe it. He said that if I participated in a drug sting that they will grant me immunity and I would have all the drug charges dropped. The other charges he could get reduced to community service or a fine.

I asked him why and he let me know that I was a first time offender and If you can convince a judge or jury of what you just told me, you are innocent and should not be saddled with a felony conviction. He said, "Your chances of beating the charge are good, especially if this guy has a history of drug possession or intent to sell known to the police. However, be aware that this may involve implying strongly that the drugs were unknown of."

I felt as if it was a done deal. He told me to get myself together and Vint will be here to pick me up. So I guess that meant that I had made bail.

The lawyer had my case extradited to Florida since I was participating in this operation. I was siked I was still going to get the best of this nigga. I guess my downfall was a blessing in disguise.

CHAPTER 27

I met with the Fed's the following day. We all sat in the lawyers' office. I was scared as hell.

Vint said that he didn't want his face shown in this situation, or his name mentioned. I agreed because we had to make a living after this regardless. I sat in the office while the officers showed me pictures of Tilak making transactions with undercover NARCS. They let me listen to voice recordings and watch videotapes. Most of it took place in his auto transportation office. The other half was from the actual warehouse where he loaded and unloaded cars.

I was relieved that my face was not in any of the evidence but they did have a witness to the event at City Place. A skinny white officer wearing glasses said after that incident they felt as if they could use me to help them instead of trying to connect me with him. I definitely agreed with that statement. They told me what I had to do and where I needed

Cheryl Sutherland

to be. They told me the time, place and what to bring. They said that I would wear a wire so just in case something goes wrong they could come in to help.

The whole problem now was what about the drugs that were already supposed to be in the trunk of the car in the garage at City Place I asked. The lawyer said that they had the car towed when I made the phone call to Vint from inside the holding cell. My man was quick on his feet. One of the federal agents came to me to tell me the plan so far. He was a cocky young fellow. His name was Agent William Trust. He had a thugged out appearance, you know, the dreads, muscular, he even wore his pants sagging. It was funny because he had some pull-out gold teeth.

I kept that joke to myself.

He told me that I had to get the drugs that were supposed to go in that car to Tilak. He said that Tilak and I had to meet face to face so that Tilak would have a sense of security with me. I nodded to show him that I was following what he was saying. He said that the drugs were evidence so don't tamper with it. I had butterflies in my stomach from the thought of seeing him in person again but I had to do it, I had to get this nigga out of my life. The will to live overpowered my fearful state of mind.

When I arrived home Vint told me to tell him all the details. I pulled one of his lines and told him that the less he know the less danger that he would be in. He laughed and slapped me on the ass. He said that he got a phone call from Tilak.

"What happened?" I asked.

"I told him that the car wasn't there when I got there. He paused for a minute and said that his driver didn't see it either. So he knew that I wasn't lying. He said that he wanted me to bring it to him."

"And...you know that I have to meet up with him face to face so let me deliver it to him."

"The Fed's gonna have your back?" he asked.

"Of course. Let me do it. I want to see his face when I hop out of the car."

"Aight. But I'm riding with you. So he won't be suspect, ya feel me."

"I see no harm in that."

We both got suited up and drove to his office. When we got there I called Agent Trust and told him that I was about to make the drop off. He said that they were right on my tail. I walked up to the office door and saw Lisa's snitching ass. I asked her if Tilak was in and she hurriedly told me no, so I called his cell phone.

"Hello." he answered.

"Tilak?" I questioned in an eerie voice.

"Yeah, who dis?"

"Tyrena." I said as I nearly pissed my pants.

"What's up, baby?"

I know he didn't. He did not just call me baby. That just made me want to shove this phone down his throat.

"Nothing much what's going on with you."

"Shit, I just been chilling."

"Well the purpose of this phone call is that I need to see you. I got the suitcase that you let me borrow and I want to return it."

"Bet. I'm at the warehouse off of Northlake Blvd."

"I'm on the way."

"Okay."

I looked at Lisa and gave her a big ass grin. I wanted to shout out that it was going down but she will feel it in a couple of hours. I called Agent Trust and told him that we had to go to the warehouse. He said that he got my back.

Vint and I drove from Juno to Lake Park in about five minutes. We pulled up to the warehouse. I called Agent Trust and he informed me that they had already surrounded the building. I looked at Vint as if this was it. Vint leaned over and gave me a kiss. He said that if it takes more than five minutes he was coming in.

I nodded.

I knocked on the door. I could hear it echo through the building. He opened the door and I was face to face with the nigga that I despised. I should've smoked before I did this. He invited me in and walked me to his desk in his office. I placed the suitcase next to the desk and sat on the desk. He sat in his chair and leaned back. I leaned in his direction and wanted to tell him bye-bye but I knew that I couldn't.

"So I hear that this is the end?" I said.

"Yep. I'm sorry for all the things I did to you. I deeply and sincerely mean it. I just lost it when you wouldn't come back to me. I started getting high on my own supply and all. I hope that you can find it in your heart to forgive me?"

"Yeah, I can forgive you."

We both stood up so we could hug each other. His hands began to slide over my body as if he was really enjoying it. I was trying to keep my cool but he was getting carried away. I tried to pull away put his grip just got tighter.

"Why the fuck you here?" he snapped "I told

Vint to bring me my package not you." He exclaimed as he tightened his bear hug.

"Vint's outside in the truck. He just wanted me to come in to make sure you was for real." I said losing breath each time I spoke a word.

Tilak loosened his grip just enough for me to get some air then resumed his hold.

"I don't believe you. All the shit I've done to you and you just gonna forgive me like that. The fuck you think I am stupid. You trying to set me up. Vint ain't in that truck."

"He is! I swear to God. He's out there, Tilak. I promise he is," I cried out. I knew that the agents would hear what's going on in this wire that I'm wearing.

Where are they?

Tilak pushed me so hard that I fell on the floor. He pulled out his old trusty murdering machine. He put it right in my face.

"I'm gonna let your tired ass walk to the door. You signal for him to come in and if he doesn't your brains will be my doormat. You get me?"

I slowly nodded.

Walking to the door I prayed that there weren't any agents standing there. I slowly cracked the door and waved for Vint to come in but nothing moved in the truck. The tints on the truck were so dark that I couldn't see if he was in the truck or not. I assured Tilak that he was in there and he just wasn't paying attention. He told me that I had four seconds. I waved hysterically but still no response.

Tilak dragged me back in the office and all I could do was cry.

"Shut up that got damn crying. Listen you little bitch you knew deep down inside that I wasn't going to stop until you were gone. Vint can't have you, he on my team, stupid. I got control of this whole situation. You still fucking that nigga 'cause the last time I saw him he said that he didn't speak to you in awhile. So what's really good? Who lying and who telling the truth?" He asked.

I hesitated to answer. I felt as if I procrastinated the situation then he'll take the time to think about what he was gonna do. That was until he cocked that gun back.

Then I snapped. "You know what's what! You told Vint that you would leave us alone if he did that run for. Why can't you be a man of your word?"

Tilak looked at me as if that was it and he wanted me off the face of this earth. He stopped when he heard the knock at the door. He walked over to the door and signaled for me to sit down in the chair. I didn't want to so I just stood there.

Vint walked in the door and asked what was

―――――― Cheryl Sutherland ――――――

the hold up.

Tilak took his gun and put it behind his back. That was the perfect opportunity. I tiptoed towards him until I was able to run up and snatch the gun out of his hand.

Vint jumped back when he saw what I was up to. He knew that I couldn't shoot that well.

I yelled out, "HELP!" that was my safe word for back up.

Tilak started to charge towards me. I closed my eyes and I squeezed the trigger.

"No, stop!" Vint yelled.

I couldn't.

I just kept pulling the trigger over and over. The shots echoed throughout the warehouse. The squad came running in. One of the detectives swung my hands up in the air and took the gun away from me. He then held me and asked me why wouldn't I stop shooting on his command.

At that point I didn't know and didn't care, I was crying and lethargic, I just couldn't get it together.

Vint ran over to me and hugged me. Everyone was quiet. Tilak was there lying on the floor in a puddle of blood. All I could do was yell out to keep him alive. After all this, I need him to suffer just like I had. Death was just too good for this bastard.

Chocolate Ty

One of the officers ran over to take a pulse. He looked around at all the merchandise and paraphernalia that was inside the facility. Everyone waited for the signal. Then he nodded his head to signal that he was still alive. The officers placed the handcuffs on him and sat him up. He looked at me as if I was wrong for what I did.

He mouthed the words "I love you" as he leaned back in agony. Everyone could tell that I was relived that he was handcuffed yet still I had a disgruntled look on my face. I knew that there was a calling on his life because out of all those shots he only got hit once in the shoulder.

CHAPTER 28

September 3rd, this was it, the big day...Tilak's sentencing.

I was excited. It took a little over a year of the bullshit and run-arounds but I didn't care. I made it through the trial, I testified against him and I sat through all the hearings that I didn't have to do but was willing to. I always wanted to go just to see Lisa's big fat ass crying over that sorry fucker and Tilak looking so good in his jumpers. I used to joke with myself about how handsome Tilak is, regardless he looked good, and Lisa did not. She had put on so much weight; I guess it was from the stress of not having a man anymore.

Vint and I got ready to go to the courthouse for the big day. Vint waited on me hand and foot. He bathed me; he put lotion on my body, he gave me a foot rub, he clothed me and put my shoes on my feet. I loved him. It was a totally different kind of love. Now that we both realized the stakes that we took for each other we knew no other could replace either one of us.

My confidence grew as we walked into the courtroom. Hand in hand. Vint had to make sure that my engagement ring was noticeable. Vint kept asking me if I was okay. I assured him that this, I definitely could handle. The officers brought Tilak out in a business suit with shackles. Tilak examined the courtroom. He laid his eyes on me. You could see the anger in his eyes as he saw my stomach poking out. Seven months pregnant and counting. I waved with my left hand so he could see the rock on my hand that his nephew bought me.

Tilak looked like he was going to be sick.

His lawyer tried his damnest to get his sentence reduced and some of the charges dropped throughout his trial but the judge wasn't having it. She put it on him. She gave a speech of "How could he torture another human being" and that he will be punished for his crimes. Just the thought of what he did to me made me bust into an emotional fit. Tilak, on the other hand, showed no emotions.

We sat through the whole trial. I was very uneasy I kept fidgeting as the judge read all the charges that he actually was found guilty of: Drug trafficking, attempted murder, kidnapping, conspiracy to traffic, murder in the first degree and

Chocolate Ty

the list went on. Just to think; for Tilak to be so smart he was really dumb. He used the same gun that he killed Pat with, pistol whipped and shot me with on him when he was arrested. How smart can you be? He had enough money to buy a different gun for each day in the month, but I guess that was his favorite. It sure made the job easier for the detectives to link it all together.

The judge read a verdict of guilty and that he has life in federal prison. I jumped up and rejoiced and I heard the music of Isaac Hayes *Walk on By* in my head.

Vint stood up and joined me in my celebration. I was reborn. This was the first day of my life.

CHAPTER 29

The last trimester of my pregnancy dragged along. I was humungous when I went into labor. I was impatiently waiting for my bundle of joy to come into the world. All the attention I received and the baby showers were a thing of the past when the contractions began. It was the most excruciating 17 hours and 34 minutes of my life. But it was so worth it at the end. I gave life to a beautiful 8lbs 6oz baby boy with black ringlets of hair. Our baby's skin was as smooth as milk chocolate. His eyes were so deep and dark that it seemed as if he could look into my soul and tell me all the struggles that I've been through just to get him here.

Also, I was blessed to have all of my family and friends there.

Vint was there too, looking like an entirely new person.

I could tell he was happy and relived all in the same breath. I loved him more than life itself. I

Cheryl Sutherland

honestly would've died for him. I'm glad I didn't have to but in the back of my mind it was always a risk that I was willing to take.

Flick was looking confused as if he couldn't believe that this was happening. It was as if he couldn't come to the realization that his homeboy is now a father. Flick was not the fatherly type. He didn't like kids at all. He also didn't like the thought of Cheryl being hugged up with Terrance on the other side of the room either. Flick was a male ho but he actually liked Cheryl. I guess karma is grey. Everything that you've done in your life from doing people wrong, to making mistakes with some one you care about, when you actually find someone that interest you that person doesn't realize it until it's too late.

Cheryl could careless about Flick now that she and Terrance had found a new love between them. Cheryl had been through a lot. Not just for me but for her self also. Cheryl told me the story on how she escaped. She ran through the woods, hitchhiked and she jumped in the car with a total stranger. She used the guy's cell phone to call Terrance and tell him to meet her in Jacksonville, from there Terrance picked her up and she made it home. I guessed Terrance really did care for Cheryl. Cheryl and I haven't talked that much because of the trial. I still love her though. We could stop communication for a minute and when we see each other it's as if nothing has changed. She realized that the struggle that here and Terrance had been through wasn't in vain. In the end Terrance was there for her in a way that she could never imagine. If it wasn't for him she would probably be in jail right now. I thanked God that she wasn't.

Shavon was there looking like new money. She acquired a couple of scars in her face from a nigga she was working. He caught on to her games and sliced her ass up. She was still a cutie and as long as her wardrobe stayed tight and teeth white she wouldn't have a problem pulling these niggas in the FLA since she decided to move down here.

My mother and her new beau were there also. Now I can see my mother being with him for a while. He was a minister and had my mom going to church and all. I can see the new being inside of her just by her smile.

This was it, my new beginning. A life that I was going to live to the fullest, a life that was gonna reap great rewards.

All of this, I was ready for...starting with my son, Sir.

CHAPTER 30

Tilak sat in his prison cell and thought about how he got played by Tyrena. He was very angry but still was in love with Tyrena. He waited two years before he decided to interrupt her life. He did it the only way that he could express himself; through pen and paper. He sat down and poured his emotions onto the ledger:

To the only woman that I ever loved,

Tyrena, I'm sorry for what I've done and all the pain that I've 'caused you. I was crazy about you, literally. I don't know what it is that you did to me but it made me flip. The only reason why I'm writing this letter and apologizing to you is because you deserve it. Tyrena you have been a blessing in disguise for all these years and I never realized it. I just want you to know that I really cared for you and I never meant to hurt you but when I saw how close you and my

─────────── **Cheryl Sutherland** ───────────

nephew were getting I just freaked out, something came over me. I didn't want him to have your heart but I guess I shoved you into that direction and the better man ended up with you.

It took me a little over a year to realize what I did to you was wrong. I mean, I knew that it was wrong at the time but I didn't feel as if I was wrong. I guess I just had to tighten up and gain the courage to let you know how special you are and that you don't have to subject yourself to anything that you don't need to. You are a decent woman and you have the ability to do what ever you want with who ever you want. Don't settle for less and don't let anyone treat you like shit either. I know that you don't need to hear this shit from someone like me but I'm saying it anyways. You da shit, you tight work so keep it up and make sure that nigga, I mean your husband don't take advantage of you. Let him treat you like a queen.

P.S. When you gonna let me stop bye and see the baby....

Love Always,
Tilak

Tilak sat back as he imagined the expression that Tyrena would have on her face as she saw the

Chocolate Ty

letter in her mailbox. He grinned to himself thinking about how sweet life would be with her one day...

———————— **Cheryl Sutherland** ————————

I hope that you have enjoyed my first novel.

    Be sure to look out for the follow up novel to Chocolate Ty entitled: "***Cannabis***".

    Also be on the look out for three more novels by me entitled: "***The Grand Hustle***", "***Blood Raw***" and "***There is a Season***".

If you have any comments or would like any information you can e-mail me at: cherylsutherland@platinumpeachpress.com or chocolatetythenovel@yahoo.com
Or you can write at:

PO BOX 18434
West Palm Beach, FL 33416

You may also visit my website at www.chocolatety.com or view my page at www.myspace.com/chocolatetythenovel or www.PlatinumPeachPress.com

    Love, Peace and Blessings to you and yours,

Cheryl

Chocolate Ty

― Cheryl Sutherland ―

DON DIVA magazine
THE ORIGINAL STREET BIBLE

To order with your credit card log on to: www.dondivamag.com or call: 877-366-3482

Order Now While Supplies Last!

Name _____
If going to an inmate confirm that magazine is allowed into jail/prison. No refunds will be given for any reason

Address _____

_____

City _____ State _____ Zip _____

Send Money Order or Institution check payment ONLY. (No Personal Checks!) to:
Don Diva Mag.
2840 Broadway,
313,
NY, NY 10025.

COVER PRICE $5.99. DON DIVA IS A QUARTERLY PUBLICATION. YOUR YEARLY SUBSCRIPTION WILL BEGIN WITH THE NEXT ISSUE AND CONTINUE FOR ONE YEAR.

[ ] Send me a yearly sub for $20
[ ] Send me issue # 6 for $8.99
[ ] Send me issue # 7 for $8.99
[ ] Send me issue # 8 for $8.99
[ ] Send me issue # 9 for $8.99
[ ] Send me issue #10 for $8.99
[ ] Send me issue #12 for $8.99
[ ] Send me issue #13 for $8.99
[ ] Send me issue #14 for $8.99
[ ] Send me issue #15 for $8.99
[ ] Send me issue #16 for $8.99
[ ] Send me issue #17 for $8.99
[ ] Send me issue #18 for $8.99
[ ] Send me issue #19 for $8.99
[ ] Send me issue #20 for $8.99
[ ] Send me issue #21 for $8.99
[ ] Send me issue #22 for $8.99
[ ] Send me issue #23 for $8.99
[ ] Send me issue #24 for $8.99

Chocolate Ty

―――― Cheryl Sutherland ――――

Mail Order Form to:
PO Box 1539
Stone Mountain, GA 30086
(678) 597-1321

Name: _____

Address: _____

City/State: _____

Zip: _____

Quantity:	Title:	Price:	Total:
	Unfinished Business By Patrick Goines	$14.95	
	Chocolate Ty By Cheryl Sutherland	$14.95	
	Queen City By Ronald Hoover	$14.95	
	Courting Miss Thang By Thomas Green Jr.	$14.95	
	Player No More By Thomas Green Jr.	$14.95	
	Tabu By Thomas Green Jr.	$14.95	
Coming Soon!!!!	**Dead Wrong** By Terrill Peterson	$14.95	

Shipping/Handling VIA US Media Mail: **FREE**
Next Day shipping: $14.95
Priority Shipping: $3.95
                           Total: $_____

Acceptable Forms of Payment:
Institutional Checks, Money Orders, All Major Credit Cards.
Please allow 5 to 7 business days to receive order.
www.PlatinumPeachPress.com